TUCKERS TURN OUT

"This is something that the FBI ought to know about."

(page 80)

TUCKERS TURN OUT

by

VIRGINIA BAKER

Author of *Crusaders on Wheels*

MOODY PRESS
153 Institute Place, Chicago, Ill.

Printed in the United States of America

Dedicated to my new nephews,
Stephen William Shoemaker
Donald John Baker, Jr.

CONTENTS

AN AFTERWARD WHICH COMES FIRST

I was walking down the Avenue the other day when I met Susan.

"Susan! Susan Tucker!" I cried. "I'm so glad to see you. I've been wanting to thank you for being in my story."

Susan grinned until the corners of her eyes were wrinkled into little crow's feet.

"And do thank Stephen and your mother and father and all the others, too," I urged, as the heavy traffic whirled past us.

Susan kept right on smiling and looking very important.

And then I said, raising my voice a little to be heard over the tooting of horns:

"When you next see friend Elizabeth, tell her 'Thank you, from the bottom of my heart.'"

For the first time, Susan turned off her smile long enough to ask:

"Who is friend Elizabeth?"

"Elizabeth," I replied, stepping aside to let four WAVES march by, "Elizabeth is my critic and faithful counsellor."

As I turned to leave, I called back over my shoulder to Susan:

"Oh, yes, and Alice Q! Please thank her, too!"

1

THE TUCKERS
OF COLLEGE HILL

"Good evening, Miss Tucker," said Dr. John Philip Tucker to his ten year old daughter, Susan, who was sitting on the steps of Big Gate across from Science Hall.

"Good evening, Professor Tucker," Susan replied with quiet dignity. "And how were the Economics today?"

"Very well, thank you. So nice of you to ask. I believe I am going your way, Miss Tucker. May I see you home?"

"Oh, yes, thank you." And Susan, grinning, leaped into her father's arms, giving him great hugs.

Hand in hand they walked through the wide, tree-shaded streets of College Hill, talking over the events of the day. At four o'clock every evening, Susan was found waiting on the campus of Russell College for her father. Indeed, it was safer to set your watch by the moment Dr. Tucker swung open the Science Hall door and strode across the walk to greet his daughter, than to trust the big college clock that solemnly bonged out the hours from the tower of the chapel. There was only one week, when Susan had the measles, that she was not waiting, but other than that, rain or shine, snow or heat, Susan was at Big Gate.

And every evening their first conversation was the same. Sometimes, it is true, the professor had to report that the "Economics" were not doing so well.

Such poor reports usually came around the time of an exciting football game.

"I received a very important letter today, Susan," said Dr. Tucker, as they neared home. "A letter which may mean a big change for all of us."

"What did the letter say, Daddy?" Susan asked, her big eyes becoming wide and round.

"I'll read it when we get home. I want Mother and Stephen to hear it at the same time. And then we shall have to decide what to do."

They turned into a driveway that led to a large white house set back from the street. Although it was just dusk, a window lamp already had been lit and was sending a pleasant welcome to them out through the trees. As they crossed the spacious porch, they could see Maggie through the window setting the table for dinner.

Susan and her father found Mrs. Tucker reading in the library before an open log fire. The walls were lined with books on shelves reaching to the ceiling. It was the Tuckers' favorite room. On winter evenings, Susan and Stephen (he was four years her elder) studied in the library while Mrs. Tucker read or mended and the professor prepared for his class the next day. It was in the library that the Tuckers spent the happiest hours together.

"Daddy has an important letter to read to us," Susan exclaimed to her mother.

"Yes," said Dr. Tucker, "I received a most interesting letter today from Washington."

"From the Capital, you mean?" asked Susan, sitting down on a stool beside her father's chair.

"Yes, from Washington, D. C., the Nation's Capital," Susan's father assured her. "Where's Stephen?

I don't want to read the letter until we are all here."

"He stayed after school to help collect and sort some scrap. He ought to be here any minute now," replied Mrs. Tucker, getting up to look out of the window.

"Oh, Stephen is always making us wait for him. He's the *slowest* thing," declared Susan impatiently. "Why doesn't he come?"

"Now, Miss Curiosity, patience, patience—" said her father as he smoothed down her hair. "This collecting of scrap for the war is quite important. Stephen is spending his time well, and we can afford to wait a little while for him."

"While we are waiting," suggested Mrs. Tucker, "you could freshen up a bit for dinner, Susan."

Susan, upstairs combing her hair, heard Stephen's bicycle scrape along the driveway. She plunged down the stairs, jumping over the last three, and landed in the center of the hall just as her brother swung open the front door and rushed in.

They met. They both fell over backwards.

"Ouch!"

"Children, children, what are you doing?" called Mrs. Tucker from the library. "It sounds as though you've broken something."

"My head," groaned Stephen. "She just broke my head. That's what broken!"

"*I* broke your head," demanded Susan indignantly, holding her hand to her forehead. "*I* broke your head? The way you came running in that front door without even looking where you were going! It was your fault!"

"Humph! Was it ladylike for you to jump down the stairs? Whoever would expect anybody to stop coming down the stairs properly and suddenly land right in the middle of the floor!"

"Susan," reminded Dr. Tucker, "I'm ready to read the letter."

"What letter?" asked Stephen, all interest.

"That's why we've been waiting for you to get home, so that we could find out, and now you've knocked my poor head so hard that I don't know whether I will be able to understand the letter when Daddy reads it. Oh, my poor head!" wailed Susan.

"If the class will come to order," said Dr. Tucker, clearing his throat, "we shall proceed."

Dr. Tucker took a letter from his pocket and opened it. He held it in his hand a moment while he adjusted his glasses.

"We know that the President has been calling men and women to Washington from all parts of our country to help in our war effort. We've been reading in the newspapers about the many jobs that have to be done: gathering scrap, rationing food supplies, producing vital materials for our soldiers and sailors and marines, and dozens of other important jobs. This letter," and Dr. Tucker paused a moment, "asks me whether I would go to Washington to take a position with the Government for the duration of the war."

The children and Mrs. Tucker sat in silence while he read the very official looking letter signed by an important person in Washington. When Dr. Tucker finished reading the only sound to be heard was the ticking of the grandfather's clock in the hall and the clatter of pans in the kitchen.

How exciting to go to Washington! To see all the wonderful buildings: the White House, the Capitol, Washington Monument, Lincoln Memorial, and all the others. But—to leave College Hill! To leave Russell College and its dignified buildings, its beautiful grounds, this lovely home—all their friends. These were some of the thoughts that went through the minds of the Tuckers as they sat around the fireplace. A charred log fell among the glowing embers, sending a shower of sparks up the chimney. After a few minutes, Dr. Tucker said:

"We must all do our part. If the Government thinks that I can be of help in some way in Washington, I believe it is my duty to go. Indeed, I'm proud to think that I am needed and that they have called upon me. Well, family, what do you think we should do?"

Mrs. Tucker spoke slowly:

"When I think of our home, the campus life, and our children's school and friends, I want to stay here. But when I think of our country, and this great war for freedom, and when I think of the people in Europe and China, indeed, the whole world, who are suffering—then I say, all of these comforts and pleasant joys of ours will wait. Let us go to Washington. Let us do our little part. When we have won this war, Russell College will still be here, and we can come back to it."

Stephen nodded seriously: "That's just the way I feel, Mom. I'm all for going to Washington."

"And so am I," added Susan. "Do you think Maggie would go with us?"

"I don't know, dear, we'll certainly ask her to go. What would we do without her?"

Just then the telephone rang and Stephen ran to answer it. They could hear his voice as he said:

"Hello.

"Yes, this is Dr. Tucker's residence—

"Yes, Dr. Tucker is here. I'll call him to the phone. Just—.

"— a message? Yes, I'll — what? I don't understand.

"Yes, I hear you, but — but, — hello — wait! — hello — he hung up! That was a funny thing," Stephen muttered, rubbing his ear.

"What? What is it Stephen?" Mrs. Tucker called.

Stephen came back to the library, his face wearing a puzzled expression.

"Some man was on the phone. He talked in a very low, funny voice. He said to give Dad a message — I couldn't quite understand it."

"What did he say?" asked Dr. Tucker.

"I'm not sure. It sounded like: 'Tell Dr. Tucker not to go to Washington.' And I think he said, 'Or he will be sorry.' And then he hung up."

"How strange," said Mrs. Tucker. "Who do you suppose it was? Why would they ever say a thing like that?"

"Maybe it was one of the college boys," suggested Susan, remembering the prank they had played last spring. One of the boys had telephoned the biology professor, pretending he was a lawyer from Chicago, and advised him of a legacy he had been left for research work with snakes. The biology professor had worried for a week for he detested snakes and had been using rabbits for years.

"I don't think so," answered Stephen slowly. "This man sounded — well, he made my neck prickle. His voice was hard and — cold."

"And you don't remember ever having heard it before?" asked Dr. Tucker.

"No," said Stephen grimly. "But I'm sure I would know it if I heard it again."

"Well, we certainly aren't going to let a mysterious telephone call keep us from going to Washington," said Dr. Tucker reassuringly. "It was probably one of the students enjoying a little joke; but there's work to be done in Washington and if we can help, to Washington we go—no matter how many people tell us to stay home."

And then they all began to talk at once. What should they take to Washington with them? What was Washington like? What kind of house would they live in? Even when Maggie announced dinner the lively discussion continued all through the meal and up until bedtime.

2
DR. TUCKER GOES TO WASHINGTON

THERE were so many things to do. College was closing for the school year, and Dr. Tucker was busy with examinations and farewells. Stephen and Susan went with Mrs. Tucker to the chapel service on Dr. Tucker's last day at the College. He was greatly loved by both teachers and students, and there were not a few eyes filled with tears at the thought of his leaving. He gave a short, simple talk to the students and the faculty about the price that our forefathers had paid for liberty and the challenge that was ours to see that freedom did not die.

And then the Tuckers rushed home to put the few remaining things into Dr. Tucker's baggage. He was to catch the two o'clock train which would get him to Washington at seven the next morning. The plan was for Dr. Tucker to get started in his new work, find a place for them to live, and write home about the things that they should bring. He would be at the station to meet them when they arrived.

His baggage, packed and strapped, was lined up on the front porch ready for Stephen to put in the back of the car to be taken to the station.

"Well," sighed Dr. Tucker, surveying his belongings with satisfaction, "I guess I've got everything shipshape."

He had barely finished speaking when Maggie, the

colored housekeeper, appeared at the front door carrying a laundry box.

"Dr. Tucker, you done forgot to put in yore clean shirts. Dey's all right here, fresh and nice. I hope yous got room for dem."

Dr. Tucker groaned. His suitcases already were so full that only by Susan standing on them had he been able to shut them. And now, where to put all these freshly laundered shirts!

"But what would you have done without any clean shirts, Daddy?" Susan asked cheerfully. "Aren't you glad we discovered them in time?"

"In time for what? I haven't any place to put them," protested Dr. Tucker. "Maggie, could you put a heavy string around that box so that I can carry it? There's no use jamming them into my suitcase and getting them all mussed up."

"Better hurry, Dad," called Stephen from the driveway. "You've only got fifteen minutes to train time, and we have to check this baggage."

"Are you sure you have everything now, John?" Mrs. Tucker inquired anxiously, straightening out Dr. Tucker's ruffled tie. "You've not forgotten anything?"

"I never knew I owned so much. My suitcases are jammed full. I just better have everything. I certainly can't carry any more."

Finally, the laundry box was securely tied and the suitcases stored in the back of the car with Susan and Stephen. Mrs. Tucker started the car rolling slowly down the driveway while Dr. Tucker waved goodbyes to the neighbors and to Maggie. As they stopped for a moment before swinging out into the avenue, Susan exclaimed:

"Wait, wait!—here comes Maggie. She's calling us."

Mrs. Tucker stopped the car and Dr. Tucker and Stephen jumped out.

Maggie came puffing up to them, waving an umbrella in one hand, a pair of rubbers in the other and Dr. Tucker's spectacle case sticking out of her apron pocket.

"You done forgot yore ovah shoes, Dr. Tucker, and yore umbrella. Paper says it been rainin' in Washington for four days—and don't look like it goin' to stop for four mo! And your spectacles. Don't know what you'd done without dem spectacles," Maggie smiled at him happily.

"Ooooohh, Maggie. I don't know whether to thank you or not. I probably need the umbrella and rubbers, all right, but where—where, Maggie—where am I going to put them?"

Mrs. Tucker started to laugh.

"The absent-minded college professor!"

"Here," said Stephen, very efficiently, "let's put the rubbers down inside the umbrella, and then we can tie the umbrella on the outside of the suitcase. I can do it on the way. We've not much time to make that train."

Maggie stood grinning after them as they again started off toward the station.

"I wonders if it's safe for him to go off to a big city all by hisself," she said.

There were about a hundred people gathered at the station to see Dr. Tucker off on the train. Some of the students had brought their musical instruments and all sorts of weird sounds could be heard as they tuned up. When the Tucker car arrived, it was immediately surrounded, the doors pulled open, and eager hands seized Dr. Tucker to help him out. Some of the students escorted Mrs. Tucker to the station while others grabbed the baggage. On the platform, they joined hands, forming a circle around the Tuckers. Cheers and yells and tooting of horns rent the air and merry voices and laughter rose in a steady hum. Dr. Tucker, very pleased and excited, kept pulling out his handkerchief and wiping his forehead.

Finally the train came roaring into the station. Passengers already on the train smilingly watched the happy group saying goodbye to the flustered man. There was a hurried last minute hug for Mrs. Tucker and for Susan and a hard handshake for Stephen. One colored porter hustled Dr. Tucker on to the train while a second porter handed up the baggage.

As the train began to puff out of the station, the "band" played the Alma Mater song of Russell College. Dr. Tucker beamed at them all out of the window, waving his hand. Susan frantically threw him dozens of kisses. Just as the last coach was passing them, a station wagon pulled up to the curb and Maggie almost fell out of it. Half-stumbling and running toward the departing train, she kept waving her arms and shouting:

"Dr. Tucker — yore money, — yore tickets! Wait — wait!"

The train's whistle shrieked merrily back at her. With streamers of grey smoke it disappeared around a curve, leaving Maggie stranded helplessly with Dr. Tucker's wallet and tickets fluttering in her hands. Mrs. Tucker, half laughing and half crying, sank down on a bench. Susan and Stephen looked blankly from Maggie to the smoke curling back from the speeding train.

3

"DEAREST FAMILY"

SPECIAL Delivery for Tuckers," shouted a postman at the front door. Susan ran to get the letter and carried it triumphantly to her mother in the library, with Stephen stepping at her heels.

"From Washington, Mother. From Daddy!"

Mrs. Tucker eagerly tore open the envelope and pulled out the bulky letter written in Dr. Tucker's large handwriting. Mrs. Tucker read it aloud:

"Washington, D. C.
Wednesday evening

"Dearest Family,

"My very best love to you all from the Nation's Capital!

"I really felt a tingle of pride when I wrote 'Washington, D. C.' at the top of this paper. This is a fascinating place, and I can hardly wait until you all come and join me here. I know that Susan and Stephen will be as thrilled as I when they walk out of the station and see the dome of the Capitol. It's great to be an American!

"But let me tell you about my trip right from the beginning. The train was about half filled, but in a few hours we began to pick up dozens of soldiers, and then later marines, and just before we got into Washington, a group of sailors got on the train. Every available seat was taken, and I believe that some even had to stand, although they walked back and forth through the train, laughing and talking, so they didn't seem to mind. They remind me of some of our boys from Russell. Stephen would have been interested in the MPs, who patrolled the train to see that the boys in uniform behaved. They weren't needed, however, for all the boys were well-behaved.

"I'm afraid I didn't sleep very well for I was too excited. The train was due to get in at seven a. m., but we were delayed at two places along the line, and so did not arrive in Washington until after nine o'clock. I guess Mother 'arrived' at seven a. m. on time (you know how she travels right along with me, in her thinking, whenever I take a trip). The reason our train was held up was to let troop trains go through. The line is so crowded and trains run so closely together, that it is necessary to switch some of them off on to sidings at times to allow others to pass. It was most interesting and was a taste of wartime emergencies.

"The railroad people have a hard job to keep everything working smoothly and without accidents. Some people on the train grumbled about being late, but most of us did not mind at all for we knew that it was due to war conditions.

"I had not been in Washington for years and years, as you know, and so was a little surprised at how big the station seemed. But even as big as it appeared, it wasn't big enough to take care of the crowds. Just wait until you see Union Station here in Washington! Uniforms everywhere, all kinds. Sailors, soldiers, marines, coastguards; English, Canadian, Free French, South American, Australian;

officers and privates and seamen. It is like a pageant. Extra ticket booths have been set up and throngs come and go all day and all night. There is a large room set aside for servicemen where they can rest and get something to eat. It is almost impossible to find a redcap. It took me half an hour to get a taxicab to take me to a hotel. And then I had to share it with two other people; one of them, an Australian army officer, and the other, a man who owns a factory which is building airplanes now.

"I spent all day today looking for a place for us to live. I'm finding out how true it is that there just aren't enough living quarters for the thousands of people coming here. Most of the real-estate people to whom I went just looked at me blankly. One or two places listed in the newspaper either were taken when I got there, or were too small, or just too dirty to consider. But I'll continue to look and to inquire around. Perhaps we may have to take a couple of furnished rooms until we can find a suitable house. I would suggest that you just bring the clothes. We'll have to leave the furniture there ready to be shipped when we find the place we want.

"Last evening, after a three-hour conference with certain Government officials, I hired a taxicab driver to drive me around the town. It has certainly grown from the pleasant, comfortable, little town that it was when I first was here. We rode down Constitution Avenue and saw the new Government buildings—tremendous, some of them covering several blocks. We drove around the base of Washington Monument. When you come, we'll go up in it. And then we went over into Arlington Cemetery, past the rows of white crosses and stones marking the last resting place of our hero dead. I saw the Tomb of the Unknown Soldier and stood beside it looking out over the great city of Washington, which the setting sun seemed to turn into a glorious tapestry. May it be a sign that our stay here will be a happy, useful one for all.

"There is so much that I want to tell you. I think that just living here will be an education for Susan and Stephen. I believe that there is much ahead for us. I am counting the days until I meet you in Union Station.

"My best love to you all—including Maggie.

"Dad.

"P. S. I suspect that Susan and Stephen are dying of curiosity to know how I managed to travel all that distance without my tickets or money. Fortunately, I met an old college friend of mine who thought I looked honest and so gave me some money.

"P.S. A strange thing happened this morning. When I opened the laundry box of my clean shirts, I found a typewritten note reading: 'You were warned once. This is the second and last warning. Don't take that Washington job.' However, it was too late for I had already accepted the job. This joker is quite a persistent chap, isn't he?"

4

ON THEIR WAY

THE Tuckers were just as eager to join Dr. Tucker in Washington as he was to have them. The next few days passed quickly. There were dishes to pack, pictures to take down, rugs to wrap for shipping, decisions to make as to whether to take or store the piano and the grandfather's clock, what to give away, and how to get all their personal belongings into three trunks.

And then Dr. Tucker wired that he could not find a house, and they might have to fit themselves into an apartment—if he could find one! That meant deciding all over again about what should be taken. If they were going to live in a small apartment, they would have room neither for their big mahogany dining room furniture, Dr. Tucker's desk, Stephen's work bench, nor for Susan's doll house. They would have to leave them all in College Hill. And, of course, they would not need a lawn mower for an apartment house!

And, when Dr. Tucker's telegram came saying that he could find only three furnished rooms which they could rent for one month, poor Mrs. Tucker had to arrange to leave all but their clothes in College Hill with Maggie. When they were finally settled in Washington, they would have to write to Maggie to ship what they could use.

"But what if we can't find any place to live in Washington?" Susan asked, a little worried.

"Don't you worry, Susan, I'll find you a nice, warm

barn to sleep in," Stephen assured her, with a big grin.

"Now, Stephen, that wasn't funny. And that's no way to talk to your sister," Mrs. Tucker reproved him.

But the way things turned out some weeks later, the Tuckers were to remember what Stephen said.

The day arrived for Mrs. Tucker and the two children to take the train to Washington. Friends went to the station with them, but this time there was no band; the students had all gone home for the summer. Nor was Maggie able to find anything they had forgotten. Indeed, they managed to board the train without any mishap.

As the train pulled out of the station, Susan and Stephen watched the town fade away from them. They had to swallow quite hard to get the lumps out of their throats. Pressing their cheeks against the window pane, the last thing they saw was the Tower Clock on the Chapel steeple.

Mrs. Tucker busied them in arranging suitcases and coats and finding a place for the lunch Maggie had packed for them. They just were settled comfortably when the train lurched around a sharp curve. Two men who had been walking down the center aisle were jolted, one of them losing his balance, fell over against Stephen. As the stranger regained his feet, he muttered something in a deep tone.

"I beg your pardon." He clicked his heels, bowed toward the Tuckers, and turned to join his companion. They hastily went into the next car.

"Mother, I think that man is a German." Stephen whispered very earnestly.

"Possibly," his mother replied quietly. "There are a lot of Germans who are naturalized and are loyal American citizens. It is no crime to be a German.

But to be a traitor to the United States is a crime."

"I'm almost certain he said something in German when he fell over against me," Stephen persisted. "Maybe he's an enemy agent."

"Oh, Stephen," protested Susan. "You're always saying things like that. He looked like such a nice man. I don't believe he could be a spy."

"You girls! You think because somebody wears nice clothes they must be all right. Why he might very well be a saboteur for all you know."

"And for all you know he might not be, so there," retorted Susan.

The train came to a stop at a country station. Some twenty soldiers were waiting on the platform with duffle bags slung over their shoulders. Stephen read a sign pointing down a side road.

"Camp Brown—2 miles. That must be where all these soldiers belong. Where are they going?"

"On furlough, I suppose," explained Mrs. Tucker.

"Just what is a furlough?" Susan wanted to know, watching the boys in uniform crowd toward the train platform.

"A furlough is 'leave' from camp, a kind of vacation that soldiers get. They are allowed to go home; or if their home is too far away, they spend their time in some nearby town. They have to be back in camp on a certain day. If they fail to return, it means discipline."

"With all these soldiers on board the train, your old German spy had better watch out," giggled Susan.

"Well, if he is a spy, I hope they catch him before we get to Washington. Then maybe you'll learn not to be fooled so easily by nice hair," insisted Stephen.

Mrs. Tucker interrupted them, "Oh, look at the lovely scenery, children!"

"I lost my grip on a cable. . . ." (page 32)

The train was rolling through the open country. From time to time they passed large farms covering many acres. Occasionally they passed through towns with factories whose tall smoke stacks poured out grey and black clouds. Hundreds of cars were clustered around each factory building. Sometimes the train slowed down to puff through a large city. Each time the train stopped, more soldiers and sailors and marines got on. Soon the train was full, and every seat in the car was taken.

During the afternoon, a sailor stopped to talk with Stephen and Susan.

"Have you been out to sea?" Stephen asked eagerly.

"Yes, I've had two trips to sea so far."

"Tell us about it," coaxed Susan. "How do you live on a boat? Did you ever get seasick?"

The sailor smiled pleasantly and told the Tuckers of his experiences living on a boat, where they slept, how they kept watch, the life boat drills, the constant hunting for enemy ships, and some of the thrilling times they had in meeting enemy warships and submarines.

Susan and Stephen listened with wonder and Mrs. Tucker stopped knitting. After a moment's pause, the sailor said:

"But that wasn't the most thrilling experience. The most wonderful thing happened to me on my last trip."

"Oh, tell us about it!" exclaimed Susan.

The sailor's face shone as he began to speak; it seemed to glow with an inner light.

"We had been at sea two days when we ran into bad weather. It was a real typhoon. You know what a typhoon is, don't you?"

"Isn't it a big wind storm that happens in the tropics?" ventured Stephen.

"That's right. It seems unbelievable—but the waves were running fifty to eighty feet high. They kept washing up over the decks and sweeping with great suction back into the sea. One tremendous wave broke over me with terrific force. I lost my grip on a cable and was swept out into that raging sea." He paused a moment as though remembering his helplessness in that terrible tempestuous sea.

"And were you drowned?" asked Susan breathlessly.

"Of course not," Stephen looked at his sister in disgust.

"I thought I was lost that time, all right. There certainly seemed to be no hope of my being saved. The seas were running high and the ship was tossing like a toy. It was impossible for the crew to attempt to save anyone washed overboard. You know, my whole life flashed before me in a moment. I thought about dying, and I was afraid to die. I was afraid to meet God. I wanted time to get ready. I cried out — it seemed my voice was lost in the howling wind — 'Oh, God — save me!' And a miracle happened. I had never believed in miracles — till that moment. A wave, running against all the other waves, picked me up and threw me right back on the deck. My breath was knocked out of me; I was stunned. But I was saved!"

"Miraculous!" cried Mrs. Tucker.

"Yes, it was a miracle, and only God could have done it," the sailor agreed. "Can you guess what day it was?"

"No, tell us," begged Susan and Stephen together.

"It was my birthday! That was some birthday present, wasn't it? But it wasn't the best birthday present I got that day."

"Why whatever could be a better birthday present than having your life saved?" exclaimed Stephen, puzzled.

At that moment two sailors came down the aisle. The train was entering a station. One of them spied their friend talking to the Tuckers and called to him:

"This is our stop, Bill. Come on."

"Coming—one minute."

Then, turning again to the Tuckers, he said: "The best birthday present I got that day was a 'born-again' birthday present."

"What is a 'born-again' birthday?" Susan asked.

"I mean the gift of eternal life. God saved my body by sending that other wave. I realized that He also wanted to save my soul. He sent His only Son, the Lord Jesus Christ, to die for my sins. That night in my hammock I acknowledged my sin and received His Son as my personal Saviour. Now I'm not afraid to meet God. He has forgiven my sins through the Blood of Christ. He gave me new life in Christ."

And then, as he stood for a moment, before joining his friends, he said:

"I hope that you know Christ as your Saviour. If you don't already know Him, you can, right now, for He is ready to save you today. Here's something for you to read. It tells you how to be saved."

And with a cordial smile, he turned and walked down the aisle of the train to his friends. The booklet Stephen had in his hand was entitled "The Gospel according to St. John."

"What an unusual young man," mused Mrs.

Tucker, staring at the doorway through which the sailor had disappeared. "I've not heard anyone talk like that since Grandmother died."

"Do you know Christ, Mother?" asked Susan quizzically.

Suddenly, Mrs. Tucker felt very much ashamed. She realized that she had failed to pass on to her children a part of the heritage that was theirs. Mrs. Tucker herself had had a Christian home. Her parents had died when she was quite young, but her grandmother had been a very godly woman. And Susan's question made Mrs. Tucker blush with shame.

"Why, Susan, don't you know? He was — He is — God's Son."

For a long time both Susan and Stephen sat quietly, still under the spell of the sailor's thrilling story. Mrs. Tucker was staring out of the window into the growing darkness. She was thinking to herself:

"I have failed my children. I never realized it. I've taken care of their physical bodies and of their minds, but I have neglected their souls, and I don't know how to make it different."

5

THE NATION'S CAPITAL

THERE he is! *There's* Daddy! *Dad-dee!* Here we are! Over here!" shouted Susan and Stephen in unison as they stepped off the train in Union Station.

Scores of people were hurrying along the platform. Some were anxiously scanning the faces of the passengers for friends and relatives; others, who had come on the train with the Tuckers, were searching eagerly through the crowd for a familiar face. Here, as on the train, were large numbers of men in uniforms. As they neared Washington, Susan had been delighted to see young women get on the train wearing the uniforms of officers in the WACs.

Dr. Tucker caught sight of his family at the same time they saw him. There was a wild scramble as Susan threw herself into her father's arms and Stephen grabbed him around the neck. Mrs. Tucker's face was wreathed in smiles.

"You are the handsomest people I've seen since coming to Washington," declared Dr. Tucker. "Where are your bags? I managed to capture a redcap on my way through the lobby. In this town that is about as clever an accomplishment as landing a 30 pound salmon without the proper equipment."

The Tuckers slowly made their way through the crowds of people into the lobby of Union Station. There the children stopped and stared. Uniforms everywhere. And strange uniforms. Porters' carts laden high with baggage. Redcaps burdened with suitcases went in and out among the hurrying people, and through it all was a rising, steady hum of many voices.

Dr. Tucker steered his family to the right toward the taxi stand. There, with several hundred others, they stood among piles of baggage and perspiring porters. A constant stream of taxicabs in double lines were quickly loaded and snorted off. The porter who had the Tucker baggage attempted numerous times to capture a taxi for his group. But each time someone else got to the cab door first, others followed, the door slammed, gears ground, and off the taxi sped.

Dr. Tucker laughed.

"You see what I mean, don't you? Did you ever see such a busy place? It's quite like a madhouse."

At last, their porter secured a cab for them.

"Where to?" the driver asked.

"Let's drive around and see some of the city first, working our way over toward Georgetown," Dr. Tucker directed.

As the cab pulled out from under the rotunda of the taxi stand, Stephen, sitting up front with the driver, gasped:

"Oh, boy! There's the Capitol! Look at that dome, Susan! And look — down there's the Washington Monument! Just like in pictures!"

Dr. Tucker winked at the taxi driver who grinned back at him in the mirror.

The taxi driver drove slowly through the congested traffic, pointing out places of interest as they went.

"There's the Supreme Court of the United States," he said, pointing to an awe-inspiring white building.

"Could we go inside?" asked Stephen eagerly.

"Yes," said Dr. Tucker. "There are certain times when you can go in and listen to cases. The Justices sit behind a long table. There are page boys, just about your age, Stephen, perhaps a little older, who stand in back of the Justices and act as messengers. To listen to a session of the Supreme Court is one of the most stirring experiences."

Next they drove slowly by the Capitol building, the children and Mrs. Tucker peering from the windows of the taxi at the long, steep flights of steps.

"It's so much *bigger* than I ever thought it would be," breathed Susan. "Why, it's tremendous."

"What it stands for is tremendous too," Mrs. Tucker said thoughtfully.

Then they drove down Constitution Avenue, past the splendid new buildings, catching a glimpse of the lower part of the Washington Monument and watching the Lincoln Memorial grow larger before them.

"To me," said Dr. Tucker, "Lincoln Memorial is the most impressive monument in the city."

"Could we go up and see it?" asked Stephen, his head half out of the cab window.

"I'd be glad to wait while you go up,'" said the taxi driver.

The Tuckers got out and slowly walked up the steps of the large white pillared monument with the magnificent statue of Lincoln in the center. A feeling of awe and quietness gripped the children and their parents. Other people were standing around looking at the figure of Lincoln, or reading the inscriptions on the side walls.

"I'm an American," said Stephen half to himself, standing very straight and tall. And his face seemed to glow with pride.

Back in the taxi, they sat in silence, as though still held by the grandeur of the memorial. As the taxi driver swung back toward the White House, once again the children were thrilled.

"See the flag on top? That means that the President is at home. When he goes away, the flag is taken down until he returns."

"To think that I'm this close to the President of the United States!" sighed Susan in ecstasy.

And then they went on to Georgetown. The driver finally stopped in front of a quaint old house, one in a long row of houses filling the block. The white colonial doorway expressed a real hospitality.

"This is where we have rooms until we can get located in our own place," explained Dr. Tucker. "This is the home of Mrs. Madison. She doesn't really rent rooms, but is willing to accommodate us until we get settled. However, next month her son's wife and three children are coming to be with her while he is overseas. We'll have to be settled in our own home by then."

"It is, indeed, a lovely old house," said Mrs. Tucker, as they entered the spacious hallway.

Mrs. Madison was a charming lady with white hair. She immediately made them welcome and at home. Stephen noticed a portrait of James Madison over the fireplace in the living room and once again felt that tickling sensation at the back of his neck as he realized that he was seeing people and places that were great in the past of his country.

That evening, Dr. Tucker took them to a quaint restaurant for dinner. They walked down a narrow alley between two towering houses to find a tearoom in the stables of a famous statesman. Of course, it had all been made over and redecorated. One would never know that it had been a stable except for the sign out front reading "The Gabled Stable."

"You might not be sleeping in a barn, Susan," grinned Stephen, "but you are *eating* in a stable."

"I think," said Mrs. Tucker, "that I am going to like Washington very much. It is really a privilege to live here, isn't it? It is certainly the center of the world these days."

"If no one minds," said Susan, "I'm hungry enough to eat a horse right now,"

6

LOOKING FOR A HOME

I'M exhausted," wailed Susan as she dropped into a comfortable chair in their temporary home.

"I'm roasting," Stephen was fanning himself with the morning paper.

"I'm almost discouraged," sighed Mrs. Tucker. "I don't know where we can look now."

Just then Dr. Tucker tapped on the door, his own special kind of a rap that the children recognized but never were able to imitate.

"What's this?" he asked, coming in with a cheery smile. "What's all this gloom I met as I came up the stairs? It's almost thick enough to cut with a knife."

"John," groaned Mrs. Tucker, "Susan and Stephen and I have been walking over this town all morning and afternoon. Not to mention every day last week and the week before!"

"I know, dear. There's nothing more tiring."

"We've climbed more stairs," continued Mrs. Tucker, "and looked at more dismal, dirty places! We've hiked out miles and miles from the car line only to find that the houses, so delightfully described in the newspaper, are overrun with termites and roaches."

"Even housing problems for termites, eh?" smiled Dr. Tucker, slumped in a chair, his legs stretched out in front of him.

"We've rushed pell-mell across town ahead of the

first evening we were here," remarked Stephen, remembering their visit to "The Gabled Stables."

"You men!" sighed Susan. "You don't even have any horse sense."

"Why, Susan," reproved Mrs. Tucker, "that wasn't at all nice."

"Oh, yes we do have horse sense," insisted Stephen, with a grin. "Horse sense is stable thinking, isn't it?"

"Stephen, Stephen, Stephen," protested his father. But they all laughed, even the taxi man.

The drive did them all good, and they turned toward home cool and refreshed. Indeed, Mrs. Tucker began to think that she might even be able to start out again the next day to look for a house.

"Perhaps," she said, "I *should* have gone out to Glen Echo to look at that house. But it seemed so far away and I'd already been out that way four times. Anyway, it is a nice cool ride on the trolley, so perhaps Susan and Stephen will go with me tomorrow."

As they got out of the cab at Mrs. Madison's front door, and saw the cheeriness of the hall lights shining out through the glass panels of the doorway, they were even more encouraged.

"I've an idea," Dr. Tucker confided. "I think there is an entire field we have neglected."

"What do you mean?" asked Mrs. Tucker. "I think I've practically combed this town."

"Yes, I know you have, but you've been looking for a particular kind of a place—a house or an apartment."

"What other kind is there?" asked Susan.

"I'll tell you tomorrow," Dr. Tucker smiled to himself. "Right now, I'm trying to use some horse sense. A bit of stable thinking, as Stephen would say."

There was a twinkle in Dr. Tucker's eyes.

7

STABLE THINKING

MRS. MADISON'S maid met Susan and Stephen and Mrs. Tucker at the front door when they returned from their trip to Glen Echo.

"Dr. Tucker just phoned," she said. "He wants you all to be ready and waitin' out front on the curb at two o'clock when he comes by for you."

"Do you mean," asked Susan eagerly, "that he's going to take us somewhere?"

"I dunno, Miz Susan, that's all he said. 'Ceptin' somethin' about 'horse sense' that I didn't quite catch," the maid answered.

When Dr. Tucker came for his family at two o'clock, he found them waiting in front of Mrs. Madison's house.

"What is this all about?" asked Mrs. Tucker.

"Where are we going?" Stephen wanted to know.

"It isn't a secret, is it?" put in Susan.

"This," laughed Dr. Tucker, "is all about our finding a place to live; we are going to Rock Creek Park; and it is not a secret."

Other than that, neither Susan nor Stephen nor Mrs. Tucker could get him to tell them any more. When they got to the edge of the park, Dr. Tucker paid the taxi man and suggested that, if he were back that way in an hour, he could pick them up. And then he led his family down the road, breathing deeply of the cooler air and enjoying the loveliness of the park on that July afternoon.

"Beautiful day, isn't it?" Dr. Tucker remarked casually, walking a little faster.

"It is indeed, but where are we going?" inquired Mrs. Tucker curiously.

"Do you like the park?" went on Dr. Tucker.

"I think it's great," said Stephen.

"I wish we could be in it all the time," added Susan.

"Like to live over this way?" continued Dr. Tucker. They all chorused "Yes".

"If you had your choice, where would you rather live? In a tent that might leak in the rain or blow down in the wind or be dismally cold in the winter? Or a nice, solid, dry building that could be heated and fixed up as snug as a bug in a rug?" Dr. Tucker kept on walking, looking at the scenery all around him, and continuing to breathe deeply of the woodsy smells.

"A house, of course," Mrs. Tucker exclaimed. "I hope you didn't take me seriously about that tent. You haven't convinced the Commissioner of Parks to let us pitch one out here, have you?"

"No, but I just wanted to be sure that you wouldn't really prefer to live in a tent," answered Dr. Tucker gravely.

"What *is* this all about?" insisted Mrs. Tucker, half frowning and half smiling at her husband.

"Well," said Dr. Tucker, "well, it's like this. For several weeks we've been looking for a house or an apartment, and we haven't found any. It seemed to me that it was time somebody got a little horse sense."

"If horse sense will solve our problem of a home, then I'm all for horse sense," said Mrs. Tucker heartily.

"And stable thinking?" Dr. Tucker asked.

"Yes, and stable thinking, too," laughed Mrs. Tucker.

Dr. Tucker had been leading his family along the road over which they had driven the day before. As they turned the next curve in the road, the palatial estate, so admired the day before, met their eyes.

"Oh!" cried Susan. "There's that lovely place."

"Do you suppose we could go in and walk around?" asked Stephen. "I'd surely like to see that swimming pool a bit closer."

"I think we could," consented Dr. Tucker in a deep voice.

He crossed to the gate that separated the private road of the estate from the public road of the park. Standing on tiptoes, he reached up to the top of the pillar. After groping a moment he brought down a key which he put in the lock of the gate.

"John!" exclaimed his wife. "What are you doing?"

"Unlocking the gate, so we can go in," he patiently explained, as he swung open the iron gate.

"There you are. Enter Tuckers!"

"But John," protested Mrs. Tucker, "this is private property! The sign over there says 'No Trespassing.'"

"Let me see," remarked Dr. Tucker, adjusting his glasses. "N-O, that spells 'No'. T-R-E-S-P-A-S-S-I-N-G, that spells 'Trespassing', doesn't it? Yes, that is exactly what the sign says. You are right. We had better hurry on in and lock the gate behind us. We wouldn't want to let in any trespassers. Step along, everybody!"

In silent amazement, Susan and Stephen and Mrs. Tucker walked obediently through the gate and watched Dr. Tucker close and lock it, and replace the key in its hiding place.

"But how did you ever know where the key was?" asked Susan.

"I was out here this morning," her father explained.

"But what were you doing out here this morning? I thought you were at the office?" asked Mrs. Tucker in surprise.

"I was at the office earlier. And then I came out here," said Dr. Tucker, starting to walk up the driveway. "Come along, dear family, I've something to show you."

The children and Mrs. Tucker followed him up the driveway. They circled the stately house and passed through an exquisite formal garden in the rear. Still with wondering surprise, they walked single file after Dr. Tucker down a little grade. In front of them was a building which once had been a stable, but which had not been used for some time. This was the stable they had seen from the road the day before and which Dr. Tucker had admired so much.

"Here, before your eyes, my family, is our future home!" Dr. Tucker bowed low and beamed at his astonished family.

"Our—our—home?" gasped Mrs. Tucker.

"Do you mean we are going to *live here*—in this building?" Susan's eyes widened.

"In *this* stable?" demanded Stephen.

"But it must belong to the people who own that house!" argued Mrs. Tucker. "How can we?"

"Maybe they won't *let* us live here," said Susan.

"But it *is* in the park, isn't it," added Stephen, looking all around him. "And right near that swimming pool, too."

Dr. Tucker took a key out of his pocket and unlocked the door of the stable.

"Welcome, Tuckers, thrice welcome, to a home discovered through horse sense and stable thinking."

8

BE IT EVER SO HUMBLE

WELL, it happened like this," explained Dr. Tucker that evening to his family as they were gathered around a restaurant table for dinner.

Dr. Tucker had refused to explain anything until this moment. He had insisted that they go through the stable, consider how it might be fixed into a real home, and what furniture they should have Maggie send from College Hill. But they could not get one word out of Dr. Tucker about how it all happened.

At first Mrs. Tucker had been rather hesitant about "moving into a stable," but as they walked from window to window and looked out into the surrounding wood, so green and shaded and cool, and saw the hills gracefully outlined against the sky, she had been persuaded. Susan and Stephen were delighted and kept rushing in and out of the place discovering new advantages to living "in the country" and calling eagerly back and forth to Mrs. Tucker to come and see.

And now, back in the city which was still smouldering after the burning heat of the afternoon's sun, hungrily eating, Dr. Tucker was confronted by six eyes expectantly waiting for him to explain all.

"Well, it happened like this," he began. "One of the men at the office, a most pleasant chap named Evans, knew that we were having difficulty in finding a place to live. This morning, after our conference in a lawyer's office, Mr. Evans mentioned to the lawyer

47

that we were looking for a place but hadn't been able to find any, and asked the lawyer if he knew of a house or an apartment that might be suitable. Well, it so happened that this lawyer, Mr. Bell, is trustee of that place in Rock Creek Park."

"How did you ever find that out?" asked Mrs. Tucker.

"That was easy," laughed Dr. Tucker. "After thinking for a few moments, Mr. Bell said that he was sorry he didn't know of any. The only empty house he knew was a big estate overlooking Rock Creek Park, but he thought that it would be too big. Besides certain heirs were considering using it. And then I had a bright idea. I asked him where it was. And when he told me—there it was all solved!"

"I don't see that," said Stephen. "What do you mean, 'all solved'?"

"Why it was very simple. I asked him if there was a stable on the place. He said there was, but that it hadn't been used for years—not since they had built the modern garages on the other side of the house. And then I just asked him right out if he would consider renting us that stable and letting us fix it up."

"I suppose he never heard of such a thing! People living in a stable," Mrs. Tucker shook her head.

"Well, at first, he didn't know whether or not I was joking. But I hastened to explain what I had in mind, and he very kindly agreed. We went right out to the place and he showed me through. He had a lot of good suggestions."

"And then you telephoned us to be ready?" finished Susan.

"That's right. And you came, and saw—and we are about to conquer one abandoned stable. The

Tuckers can do it all right. There's nothing like a little problem such as this to bring out the Tucker-stuff
in us, eh, children?"

Susan and Stephen both agreed.

"You can't keep a good Tucker down," said Stephen.

"We Tuckers can turn out and do the job, all right,"
added Susan with confidence.

"There is one thing we shall have to do even before
we start cleaning it up," continued Dr. Tucker. "The
place must be overrun with rats. Just as we stepped
into the stable this morning, Mr. Bell dropped a pack-
age—it sounded like a ton of bricks—and there was a
pattering overhead. I suppose they do have a lot of
trouble with rats in the park. The Zoo being there undoubtedly draws them."

Susan shuddered: "Rats!"

"Aw, Susan, rats wouldn't hurt you!" Stephen said
in disgust at his sister's fastidiousness.

"We certainly will have to get rid of them," agreed
Mrs. Tucker. "I wouldn't think of moving into a place
that had rats."

"I'll call an exterminator and ask him to take care
of that job," Dr. Tucker assured them all.

"Do you suppose it will take long?" asked Susan.

"Oh, I wouldn't think it would take longer than 48
hours. If he uses some kind of chemical and jams up
the holes, it may need a little while to air out, but not
too long."

"He could leave all the windows open," suggested
Mrs. Tucker.

The next morning Dr. Tucker called an exterminator
and arranged with him to go to the stable immediately
and get to work. He was to telephone the Tuckers

when he finished and tell them what kinds of pests he had found.

When the exterminator called that evening, Stephen took the message:

"Will you tell Dr. Tucker that I went over the entire building. I couldn't find any traces of rats, except one small hole where they might have come in which I plugged up. However, just to be on the safe side, I sealed the place and fumigated it for a few hours and when I came away I left all the windows open, just as Dr. Tucker told me to do. I think it ought to be sufficiently aired out by morning."

That evening the Tuckers walked through the tree-lined streets of old Georgetown, enjoying the cool night air after another scorching day. Suddenly Mrs. Tucker stopped in the middle of the sidewalk:

"I simply *will not* use that word again," she exclaimed aloud, as though continuing an argument with herself.

"Use what?" asked Susan, puzzled, and looking at her mother.

"What word?" laughed Dr. Tucker.

"Why the word 'stable', of course."

"Whatever a r e y o u talking about, Mother?" Stephen, who had been walking ahead, joined the group which had stopped in front of a driveway, quite blocking both it and the sidewalk.

"It just isn't right to call our house a stable and I won't do it," continued Mrs. Tucker firmly.

"But it *is* a stable, or at least it used to be," said Stephen.

"But we are *not* going to live in a stable," insisted Mrs. Tucker.

"Oh, Alice!" groaned Dr. Tucker, "you are not going to back out now, are you?"

"Oh, no," she assured him. "I'm not refusing to live in that — that — place — but I am absolutely refusing to call it a — stable. If we move in, it will cease to be a stable. It will become the Washington home of the Dr. John Philip Tuckers, of College Hill."

"I see what you mean, Mother," Susan said seriously. "It doesn't sound nice to talk about living in a stable. What would Maggie think if we wrote her that we were moving into a stable? I don't think she would want to come to Washington. I know I wouldn't if somebody told me that."

"That's just what I mean," agreed Mrs. Tucker.

"But it still is a stable," Stephen insisted.

"*Was* a stable, Stephen," corrected his mother. "But now it is our home. Oh, I don't mean that I'm ashamed of living there! I'm really thankful for it. And I'm sure that we can make it very comfortable. It's — it's a — haven to us."

"Why don't we call it that, then?" asked Dr. Tucker.

"Call it, what, Daddy?" Susan wanted to know.

"Haven, Tuckers' Haven—or Haven House. Something like that," suggested Dr. Tucker.

"Haven House! I rather like that, John," Mrs. Tucker repeated the name to herself several times.

"How about it, Tuckers? Do you like it?" Dr. Tucker called for a vote.

"I think it's lovely," exclaimed Susan.

"Sounds all right to me," agreed Stephen.

"Then Haven House it shall be," announced Dr. Tucker. "Let the word stable cease to be attached to the Tucker home. Henceforth, use only the name Haven House."

9

STRANGE HAPPENINGS IN
THE STORM

BUT that evening, just as the Tuckers were ready to go to bed, a storm began to blow.

"All the windows are open at the stable — I mean at Haven House," exclaimed Mrs. Tucker in dismay.

"The rain will come in and soak the whole place," cried Susan.

"The storm might blow over," said Dr. Tucker, looking out of the window. "A little wind doesn't always mean rain."

But it didn't blow over. Dr. Tucker kept peering out of the window at the flashes of lightning, and the sound of thunder seemed to be coming nearer and nearer by the moment.

"Stephen," he said, "it looks as if you and I will have to get ourselves out there and close those windows. I only hope we can find a taxi."

"We'll have to get our car from home," said Mrs. Tucker. "I didn't know how much we would miss it."

While Susan telephoned for a taxi, Stephen and Dr. Tucker got into their raincoats and boots. They had only one umbrella between them. The wind blew swirls of dust through the air and the street lights swayed back and forth casting eerie shadows on the darkened avenue. Mrs. Tucker and Susan stood shivering in the doorway as they watched Stephen and Dr. Tucker wait at the curb for the taxicab.

"This is going to be a real storm, all right," said Mrs.

Tucker. "Do be careful. I only hope that you get there before the storm breaks. And hurry back. We won't go to bed until you come."

The cab finally arrived. The storm broke before they got to the park. The rain fell in such force that the cab had to creep along for the road could only be seen a few feet ahead of them.

"If it had only held off for a few minutes longer," groaned Stephen.

They had to direct the driver by visible land marks for they had not yet learned the names of the roads. When they turned off the main road onto the private driveway, the cab sank into the soft earth.

"Wait here for us, please," instructed Dr. Tucker. "We'll not be gone more than ten minutes."

It took a few moments for Dr. Tucker to grope in the dark for the key on the gate post ledge. The rain beat down upon them and was running in rivers off their hats. Their feet kept sliding in the mud. Finally, the gate was unlocked. Dr. Tucker and Stephen began to run up the driveway and around the big house. They could see the open windows of the stable ahead of them as a brilliant flash of lightning zigzagged across the sky. A bolt of thunder seemed to shake the very earth under their feet. There was another wait at the front door while Dr. Tucker fumbled with a key, trying to fit it into the lock.

"You shut the windows down here, Stephen. I'll tend to those upstairs," Dr. Tucker shouted above another rumble of thunder.

Stephen ran from window to window, slamming them shut and locking them. Occasionally his feet slipped in the water on the floor. Suddenly, as he pulled down the last window, he heard a commotion upstairs. Stephen stood still, listening.

A sound of scuffling, thumping of feet, footsteps running, a muffled shout that sounded like his father's voice. Stephen went cold all over. Something was wrong with his father. He ran to the stairs. As he leaped up two steps at a time, someone started coming down from the top.

"Father," shouted Stephen. "Are you all right?"

The figure coming toward him didn't answer. Stephen stopped, and called again.

"What's wrong? Are you all right? Dad!" The darkness was suddenly pierced by a flash of lightning. Stephen saw two people on the stairs. The next instant they had bolted into him. Stephen fell over backwards and bumped head first down the stairs. Feet flew by him out the front door. Stunned, for a moment he could not move, then shaking with fright and gasping for breath he got to his feet.

"Dad! Where are you?"

Stephen groped his way up the stairs. He felt a sharp pain in his arm. At the top of the stairs, he stopped a moment and called again:

"Dad, where are you? Are you all right? What happened?"

There was a groan from his left. Stephen saw something move in the corner of the room. In a moment Stephen was at his father's side. A flash of lightning showed his father lying on the floor, with something white covering his face. Stephen yanked it off, and lifted his father's head from the floor. He felt a lump on his father's forehead. Dr. Tucker groaned again.

"Dad, speak to me! Are you hurt?" begged Stephen, with a cold fear gripping his heart.

"I'm — I'm all right. Got — got a — little bump — on my head."

Stephen shoved up the nearest window and the rain poured in. As it struck Dr. Tucker's face, it seemed to revive him. Slowly he sat up.

"Where did they go?"

"Two people ran downstairs and out the door," answered Stephen. "What happened, anyway?"

"I don't know exactly. I was closing the windows over there and suddenly I heard a noise behind me. I half turned—and somebody jumped on me. We scuffled, but just as I tried to shout, something hit me. I saw stars! My head!" Dr. Tucker felt his head, rubbing his fingers lightly over the bump.

"Who were they?" asked Stephen. "They knocked me back down the stairs. I think I hurt my arm."

"They were probably tramps. I guess they found the windows open and thought it would be a dry place to spend the night. When we surprised them, they gave us a bit of fight and ran off."

"They certainly were rough," remarked Stephen, wiggling his arm and screwing up his face with pain.

"We'd better close the rest of these windows and get on home. Mother will be worrying about us." Dr. Tucker got to his feet and leaned against the wall for a moment. "Where's my hat? Can you see it, Stephen?"

They were a sad looking pair as they closed and locked the remaining windows. Securely fastening the outside door, they hurried toward the road where they left the taxi.

"Guess the cabman turned his lights out," said Stephen, as they came in sight of the road and could not see the taxi. A flash of lightning gave them a full view.

"Why, he's gone!" exclaimed Stephen.

"No!" answered Dr. Tucker in unbelief. "He can't be. I plainly asked him to wait. Maybe he went down the road to turn around where the ground isn't so soft. We weren't gone more than five minutes longer than we said."

While Dr. Tucker locked the gate and returned the key to the ledge, Stephen looked up and down the road. There was no taxi. It had gone off and left them in the lonely park in the storm.

"Well, Stephen, I hope you feel like a four mile hike in a drenching rain, accompanied by an orchestra of thunder and an off-and-on flashlight of lightning. Here we go, Son, hike!"

With the cool rain beating on their faces, they began to splash their way through the stormy night toward home.

10
INVESTIGATION

ISN'T there a car coming yet?" asked Mrs. Tucker, anxiously.

Susan, standing in front of the window which overlooked the street, pressed her nose against the pane and peered eagerly out into the night.

"No, nothing in sight. Yes, here comes one."

Mrs. Tucker ran to the window. But the car whirled by, splattering through the puddles and throwing water into the air. Mrs. Tucker looked at the clock on the mantle. One-thirty in the morning!

"Oh, dear, something dreadful must have happened to them. They surely couldn't take this long to make that trip out and back. What should we do? I wonder if we should call the police or the hospitals. There might have been an accident."

Suddenly Susan exclaimed:

"Here come two people, walking."

Mrs. Tucker and Susan watched the two dark forms approach. The two figures, obviously drenched, turned up the steps of Mrs. Madison's house.

"It's Daddy and Stephen!" Susan shouted. Mrs. Tucker and Susan rushed down the stairs. They arrived at the front door in time to fling it open for the rain-soaked pair.

"Where have you been?" demanded Mrs. Tucker in relief to see them. "We have been so worried about you."

Mrs. Tucker helped them out of their dripping coats

57

and hats and boots in the vestibule, while Susan ran upstairs for newspapers in which to carry the wet garments lest they trail water through Mrs. Madison's lovely hall.

"Walking home," grinned Stephen, as he mopped his wet face with his already damp handkerchief.

"Walking in this rain?" asked their mother in astonishment. "Couldn't you find a taxi?"

"We thought we had one," explained Dr. Tucker. "But he didn't wait for us. We had to walk into Connecticut Avenue. All the stores were closed so we couldn't phone for a cab, and since none came along we had to walk all the way home."

As Stephen stooped to pick up his boots, he winced and held his arm.

"What's wrong with your arm, Stephen?" Mrs. Tucker asked quickly.

"Nothing — that is — hardly anything," he brushed her question aside.

"Have you hurt it?" she insisted with concern.

"A little, I think," he reluctantly replied.

"Come on upstairs, and let me look at it. We've made a fire for you. You both must be chilled to the bone."

Upstairs, under the brighter light, Susan caught sight of the lump on her father's forehead.

"What made that bump on your head, Daddy?" she asked, standing on tiptoe to get a better view of the now large swelling on Dr. Tucker's head.

"You two have had an accident, now haven't you? Don't put me off any longer. I insist on knowing," Mrs. Tucker said firmly.

"Nothing very much," Dr. Tucker assured her. "A couple of tough tramps were trying to keep dry in the stable. We seemed to have interrupted their comfort."

"Tramps!" exclaimed Susan. "What did you do to them?"

"We didn't do much to them. But they surely seemed to get in a lot of blows at us," answered Stephen grimly.

"Now begin at the beginning, and tell us all about it," urged Mrs. Tucker, pushing chairs up to the fire-place for them.

Between the two of them, the weary and wet pair told of their encounter with the two men in the dark stable; and how, when they returned to the road, the taxi had disappeared and so there was nothing to do but to walk home.

"Do you think it will be safe to live out there with tramps around?" asked Susan, a little worried.

"Of course," said Stephen, a bit impatiently. "Tramps aren't always around. Lots of people live out there. After all the place *has* been empty for a long time. When we move in, there won't be any tramps near the place."

"I hope not," said Mrs. Tucker, a little doubtfully. "Do you really think we ought to consider moving out there? One can't have tramps going about hitting people on the head and throwing them down the stairs, you know. Isn't it a bit risky?"

Dr. Tucker laughed.

"My dear, it is just as Stephen said. Once we move in and they see lights and people, they certainly won't be bothering the place any more. There's nothing to worry about. It will be as safe as living in the White House."

"Did the rain soak up the floors very much?" asked Susan.

"We couldn't tell in the dark. Of course, we should have taken flashlights. Perhaps if we'd had flashlights, the tramps might have seen us coming and jumped out a back window. Next time we go prowling around in the park, we'll take a light with us, you can be sure of that."

"Well," said Mrs. Tucker, "we'll have to go out there in the morning and see how things are. And the first thing tomorrow, we must wire Maggie. I do hope her nephew Silas will be able to bring her in the car. I shall certainly be glad to get settled. But, oh my, it *is* going to be such a lot of work!"

The next morning, Dr. Tucker's swollen head was black and blue; and Stephen's arm still throbbed. But nothing could have kept them from returning to the stable. In front of the big gate, they could see the marks of the taxi and their own footsteps. While Dr. Tucker was opening the gate, Stephen carefully examined the ground.

"This looks funny," he said thoughtfully.

"What does," Susan asked, all curiosity.

"Here are our footsteps," Stephen pointed out. "There's where we went in, and here they are coming out. There's mine going out to the road to look for the taxi and there's Dad's coming after me."

"I don't think that's very funny," remarked Susan, turning away.

"Watch out where you're stepping," Stephen yelled.

Startled, Susan cried: "Stop frightening me. I thought surely the tramps were coming back."

"Children, this is no time for fussing," Mrs. Tucker scolded.

"But Dad," insisted Stephen, calling to his father. "Look at these two pairs of footprints. They aren't ours for they weren't made by rubber boots. They come out of the gate here and go right to where the taxi was, and there they end."

"They might have been made this morning by someone from the big house," said Mrs. Tucker. "Let's be getting on so you can get back to the office, John."

Dr. Tucker was looking at the footprints Stephen had pointed out.

"They are filled with water, like those of ours. It does seem as though they were made during the rainstorm. And the rain stopped last night before we went to bed." Dr. Tucker seemed to be thinking out loud.

"And it didn't start until we were almost here," Stephen said excitedly. "The ground wasn't soft until after it had been rained on."

"That's right, Stephen," Dr. Tucker said. "You know what it looks like to me? Those two tramps came down here and took our taxicab."

Mrs. Tucker smiled. Tramps riding in taxicabs! What next! They sounded like a couple of detectives.

"I wouldn't think a cabman would take tramps as passengers, would you?" asked Susan.

"No, I wouldn't," her father agreed. "But the tramps might have *forced* him to do it."

They found that the rain had done very little damage to the floors of their new home. Upstairs, Dr. Tucker explained how the tramps had jumped on him the night before. Stephen picked up something white from the floor.

"Here's your handkerchief, Dad," he said, handing it to his father.

"Not mine. I never had one like that. Are you sure it isn't yours?"

"It doesn't belong to any of the Tuckers," said Mrs. Tucker, examining it. "It has a 'W' in the corner."

"Then it must belong to the tramps," exclaimed Susan, looking over her shoulder.

"First your tramps ride in taxis," protested Mrs. Tucker, "and now they carry clean white handkerchiefs. They certainly aren't like any tramps I've ever heard about!"

"It is strange," agreed Dr. Tucker thoughtfully. "But we can't be worrying about it now. We've got much more important things on hand."

"Still," said Stephen, "it does seem funny, doesn't it? I'd like to know more about those tramps, wouldn't you?"

11

ANCHORED AT LAST

FOR the next several days Haven House had been the scene of scrubbing, sweeping, and cleaning. A long procession of help, colored and white, had come and gone, and left behind them a spick-and-span, freshly painted, and brightly decorated house. The oaken panelled walls had been polished to a beautiful finish, and the hardwood floors had been sanded, scraped and varnished until they were like mirrors.

The second floor of the stable, once used for servants' quarters, already was divided into rooms. But the first floor had to be remodelled according to plans the Tuckers had sketched during those last evenings at Mrs. Madison's home. The exterior of the stable had been given a coat of paint, and the large double doors, which took up nearly the entire front of the house, had been sealed and nailed fast. Only the small door to the right had been retained for the Tuckers' front entrance. And now the last of the carpenters and painters and plumbers had departed.

Maggie and the car, driven by her nephew, Silas, had arrived early one morning, and that same afternoon the moving van had swept into the driveway bulging with the Tuckers' possessions. Silas stayed on for a few days to arrange the furniture and clean up the yard; and, after helping Stephen put up a rustic sign "HAVEN HOUSE" above the front door, Silas had returned to College Hill.

When Dr. Tucker came home the next evening, he found Mrs. Tucker lounging wearily in an armchair and Stephen and Susan rearranging their books.

"I really think we are settled at last," Mrs. Tucker greeted him. "And it *is* cozy, isn't it?"

"I honestly don't think we could have found a nicer place to live," agreed Dr. Tucker, kissing his wife affectionately. "And you and Susan and Stephen have turned it into a little palace."

"And Maggie and Silas, too," Susan reminded him.

"It is pretty neat, isn't it," Stephen looked around the room admiringly. "Not a bad stable."

"Oh, Mother," wailed Susan, "when is he ever going to learn?"

Mrs. Tucker cast a frown toward Stephen. "Stephen?"

"Well," Stephen pouted. "I can't see anything wrong with a stable, especially a nice clean one like this."

"But," cried Susan, "this *isn't* a stable any more."

"Oh, all right," grudgingly agreed Stephen. "You girls! I'll call it Haven House if it will make you happier." As he got to his feet, he added, "But it is a stable."

"Not to change the subject," Dr. Tucker broke in, "but it looks as though we have neighbors in the big house."

"Yes, they moved in today. I must go and call on them. Or perhaps since we are somewhat of squatters on *their* land—do you suppose we ought to wait until they call on us?" Mrs. Tucker asked her husband.

Before they had decided the answer to that question, one of the new neighbors answered it for them. After dinner there was a tap at the front door and

Susan ran to open it. Standing at the door was a plumpish, pleasant lady with graying hair. She smiled at Susan.

"Good evening, I'm Miss Able, from the big house." She pointed toward the mansion across the lawn. "Miss Sarah Able."

"And I'm Mrs. Tucker," welcomed Susan's mother, arriving at the door in time to hear Miss Able's introduction. "Do come in Miss Able. We were just talking about calling on you."

In the living room, Mrs. Tucker presented her family to Miss Able, and after proper greetings they all found comfortable chairs.

"We want to thank you, as well as Mr. Bell, for letting us move in here." Dr. Tucker's voice conveyed the appreciation he felt. "It's been a haven to us. Indeed, as you perhaps noticed, we've named it Haven House."

"On the contrary, we are the ones to thank you," graciously answered Miss Able. "Mr. Bell has been wanting us to enjoy this lovely estate for a long time. But since there are only my two sisters and I, we hesitated to live so far away from neighbors and in such a big house. When Mr. Bell told us about you folks, that settled our problem. We packed up and came right out. Isn't it delightful to live right in the park?"

"We're really becoming students of nature," laughed Mrs. Tucker. "Stephen got some manuals on wild flowers and birds from the public library, and we've all been learning. I'd never known before how much I was missing!"

For another fifteen minutes they talked pleasantly about the estate and the attractive remodelled stable. As Miss Able was leaving, she pressed upon them all

an invitation for tea very soon. Susan walked with
Miss Able up the winding path to the knoll of the hill
on which was perched the big house. It was just growing dark. All around them was the sound of twittering
birds settling down for the night. The quietness of
the evening was broken only by an occasional toot of
a horn as traffic whirled down distant Connecticut
Avenue.

Susan said impulsively:

"I think this is the most beautiful place in all the
world."

"It is, indeed," agreed Miss Able. "My cousin
called it Broad Acres. God made His world very
beautiful, didn't He?"

They had arrived at the side entrance of the big
house. Susan stopped for a moment, kicking pebbles
in the driveway. After a pause, she asked shyly:

"How did God make the world?"

"It's a very wonderful story, Susan. The Bible tells
us about it."

"I — I wish you would tell me about it sometime —
when you aren't busy, I mean," Susan added quickly.

"Susan, I would rather do that than anything else
I can think of," Miss Able answered cordially.

"I know the world is awfully old," Susan ventured,
"millions and millions and billions of years old. No-
body really knows exactly how old, but it has been
ever so long since our world fell off the sun. We
studied about it in school."

"Really?" Miss Able asked very seriously. "But
you know that isn't what the Bible tells us. God says
that it happened very differently. As for me, I believe
what God says. You see — God was there when the
world was made, indeed, He made it Himself. Surely

He must know just how it all came into being. Wouldn't you think so?"

"Why, yes," agreed Susan thoughtfully. "If God made the world, He must know all about it."

"And God *did* make it. That's the wonderful part of it. When we go to the Bible for our answers, there are no 'ifs'. We know because God makes it so plain."

"Do you own a Bible, Miss Able?" Susan asked with interest.

"Yes, indeed. It is my most treasured Book." Miss Able paused a moment and glanced at her watch. "It's quite early yet, Susan. If your mother wouldn't mind, we might read some of the creation story this evening. Would you like to?"

"Oh, yes," exclaimed Susan eagerly. "I'll run down and ask Mother. I won't be a minute."

Miss Able watched Susan skip down the path toward Haven House and then went into the sunroom to arrange some chairs and to switch on some lamps.

"Mother," cried Susan, bursting into the living room where Mrs. Tucker was watching Stephen and his father play a game of chess. "Could I go up to Miss Able's for a little while? We are going to read a story —about how God made the world."

"Are you certain you aren't bothering Miss Able?" asked Mrs. Tucker. "They just moved in today—and must be dreadfully busy."

"Oh, I'm sure she wants me," Susan urged. "We're going to read the Bible. She owns one, Mother."

"How nice," Susan's mother answered. "Yes, you may go — but don't stay too long."

Susan bounced out the front door. Dr. Tucker watched her: "The Bible, eh?" he said thoughtfully.

"Your move, Dad."

12

"HE MADE THE STARS ALSO"

MISS Able was waiting at the door for Susan. A lamp sent a cheery light out into the warm summer evening. A table, on which was lying an open Bible and a large stationery box, and two chairs had been placed near a lamp. Miss Able handed Susan the Bible.

"The creation story is at the very beginning of the Bible in a book called 'Genesis.' Would you like to read aloud Susan?"

"All right," Susan answered. "Is it very hard?"

"No, God made His Book so simple that even little children can understand it."

"Where do I begin?" Susan asked.

"At the first verse," Miss Able pointed out. "I think it would be nice if we talked about the verses as we went along, don't you?"

Susan read:

"In the beginning God created the heaven and the earth. And the earth was without form, and void; and darkness was upon the face of the deep. And the Spirit of God moved upon the face of the waters. And God said, Let there be light: and there was light. And God saw the light, that it was good: and God divided the light from the darkness. And God called the light Day, and the darkness he called Night. And the evening and the morning were the first day."

"Let's stop for a moment and see what God is telling us in these verses," suggested Miss Able, opening the box and taking out some plain white sheets of paper and some colored pencils. "What does He say in that first sentence?"

"It says that God made the heaven and the earth," Susan read, watching Miss Able who was drawing a large circle on a sheet of white paper.

"Let's call this plain white circle the earth as God made it. God is perfect, and everything He makes is perfect. And so His world was perfect. What does the verse say next?"

"Well," said Susan slowly, "it says something about the earth being dark."

Miss Able drew another circle and filled it in with black crayon, like this:

"This earth looks very different, doesn't it?"

"Yes," Susan agreed. "What does it mean?"

"It means that something happened to the earth that God had made perfect, and it was spoiled."

"What spoiled it?" Susan was all interest.

"The Bible tells us that an angel, named Lucifer, rebelled against God and that God had to cast out

Lucifer and with him all the other angels who followed

his disobedience. So this perfect earth God had made
was ruined when Lucifer and his angels sinned. But
God did not let His creation stay in that darkened
condition."

"What did He do?"

"He tells us in these verses. See if you can find it."

Susan read silently for a moment.

"Is it where God said, Let there be light?"

"Yes, and what happened?"

"There was light," Susan answered triumphantly.

Miss Able drew a third circle.

"What did God do with the darkness?"

Susan considered it.

"He separated it. He put one half on one side and
the other half on the other side."

Miss Able drew a line through the circle from top to
bottom and began to color the left half of the circle
black and the right half yellow.

"What did God call the light?"

"Day."

"And what did He call the darkness?" she asked.
"Night."
"And so we have the first day. Let's read on, Susan."
Susan read:
"And God said, Let there be a firmament in the
midst of the waters, and let it divide the waters from

the waters. And God made the firmament, and divided the waters which were under the firmament
from the waters which were above the firmament: and
it was so. And God called the firmament Heaven.
And the evening and the morning were the second
day."

Miss Able drew still another circle.

"Now, how shall we divide this circle?"

Susan was beginning to understand, and she studied
carefully the verse she had just read.

"There's a heaven. Is that what we call sky?"

"That's right. We'll color that a light blue. What
is on either side of the sky?"

"Water?"

"Yes. So in this picture we have the firmament

or heaven with water above it and water below. What is the water above?"

"Clouds, I guess."

"Exactly. Let's color the water a darker blue."

"I often wondered how the sky got up there," Susan remarked. "And what held it in place."

"Only God could have put it there, and only God can hold it there. We read in the New Testament that it was the Lord Jesus Christ — who is very God — who made the heaven and earth and who holds it in place. We have a wonderful Saviour, Susan."

"There was a sailor on the train who told us about Christ," Susan said earnestly. "Tell me some more about Him."

"He is the Son of God. And He made the world and all that there is in it. And when the world forgot God and went far away from Him, the Lord Jesus Christ came into the world to bring men and women and boys and girls back to God. It is a marvelous story, Susan. One day very soon we'll read about it together."

"I'd love to read it. Is it in this Bible, too?"

"Yes, and there are many, many other stories. You'll love them all, Susan."

"What did God make next? Should I read some more verses?"

"Read down to the end of the third day."

Following along with her finger, Susan read:

"And God said, Let the waters under the heaven be gathered together onto one place, and let the dry land appear: and it was so. And God called the dry land Earth; and the gathering together of the waters called he Seas: and God saw that it was good. And God said, Let the earth bring forth grass, the herb yielding seed and the fruit tree yielding fruit after his kind, whose seed is in itself, upon the earth: and it was so. And the earth brought forth grass, and herb yielding seed after his kind, and the tree yielding fruit, whose seed was in itself, after his kind: and God saw that it was good. And the evening and the morning were the third day."

"We'll need another circle," Miss Able drew it as she spoke. "We'll want clouds, heaven, and water in this one also. And what is the new thing that God brings into the picture?"

"Fruit trees and grass," Susan said scanning the verses.

"Floating on the water or in the clouds?" laughed Miss Able.

"No, on the earth. I guess the earth is first," Susan corrected herself with a grin.

"And what does God call the waters?"

"Seas," answered Susan promptly.

Miss Able finished putting these various things in the circle.

"It is getting late. Perhaps we should stop for this evening," Miss Able suggested, looking at her watch.

"Oh, couldn't we read just a little bit more!" Susan pleaded. "We can do it quickly — Mother won't mind; I'm sure she won't."

"Well, just one more day, then. I think we can use this same picture too, and that will save time."

Again Susan turned the Bible toward the lamplight and read:

"And God said, Let there be lights in the firmament of the heaven to divide the day from the night; and let them be for signs, and for seasons, and for days, and years: and let them be for lights in the firmament of the heaven to give light upon the earth: and it was so. And God made two great lights; the greater light to rule the day, and the lesser light to rule the night: he made the stars also. And God set them in the firmament of the heaven to give light upon the earth, and to rule over the day and over the night, and to divide the light from the darkness: and God saw that it was good. And the evening and the morning were the fourth day,"

"What do we add to our picture now?" Miss Able asked.

"Does this mean the sun — and the moon?"

"And — what else?"

"And the stars! He must be a very great God to make all those things," Susan marveled.

Miss Able put down her crayon, and Susan admired the picture.

"Which does God tell us was first, Susan? The sun or the earth?"

Susan thought a moment, and then said: "The earth, doesn't He?"

"Yes. So it couldn't be true that the earth fell off the sun, when the sun hadn't been set in the heavens until after the earth appeared, could it?"

"Why, no!" Susan's eyes became very large. And then after a few moments: "Doesn't my teacher know that the earth was first?"

"I'm afraid your teacher does not believe it," Miss Able said sadly.

"But why not? If it's true?" Susan wanted to know.

"Because your teacher does not believe God's Word. There are some people — too many of them — who turn away from God and His Word and who try to think up their own explanations. But we must not talk any longer — it is time for you to go home. I don't want your Mother to worry about you. Come back again and we'll finish this wonderful story."

"Oh, I will!" affirmed Susan, "I will. I want to know all about it. Isn't it — wonderful?"

"Yes it is wonderful. We have a wonderful God. And He sent His wonderful Son to be our Saviour — to be your Saviour, Susan. Here's a Scripture verse that I want you to learn: 'For God so loved the world that he gave His only begotten Son that whosoever (that means you, Susan Tucker) believeth in Him should not perish, but have everlasting life.' Remember it, Susan. Don't ever forget it."

As Susan skipped down the path toward Haven House she looked up into the sky with an awe she had never felt before. There was no moon shining but the heaven was dotted with stars. For a moment she stopped and gazed in silence.

"God made it all. The moon and the sun—and the stars also."

13
THE PARACHUTE

IT seems to me," said Dr. Tucker, "that a Saturday afternoon like this was made for a hike."

"I second that," said Stephen, jumping to his feet. "Let's go."

"Let's walk over toward that hill there," suggested Susan, pointing to the center of the park.

"Just give me one minute to put on walking shoes, and I'll be with you," called Mrs. Tucker, running upstairs.

In a few moments they were all ready to go.

Leaving the road, they cut across the unpathed rocky hill on the other side. As they began to climb the hill, a collie dog came bounding after them.

"What a pretty dog," cried Susan. "Oh, I wish we had one."

"Where would we put such a big dog in our little house?" laughed Dr. Tucker.

"He seems to like us," said Stephen. The dog frolicked playfully, running alongside of them as they puffed up the hillside.

When they neared the top, the collie ran on ahead and was lost from sight.

"Oh, he's left us!" cried Susan. "I wanted him to stay."

"He may be back," Dr. Tucker said. "He probably caught a rabbit smell and has gone off to investigate."

A few minutes later they saw him up ahead of them in a little clearing, digging in the ground.

"Ha," said Stephen, "he must have remembered he buried a bone, and is checking up to see if he still has it. Dogs are smart, all right."

The dog dug frantically in the soft earth which was covered with a layer of leaves. Suddenly he stopped digging and came trotting toward them with a bone in his mouth.

"Good dog," shouted Dr. Tucker, stroking the dog's head affectionately.

"Oh, Mother! Miss Able asked me to go to Sunday School with her tomorrow morning." Susan remembered her invitation. "May I go?"

"Why, yes, dear. I think it would be nice. I wish Stephen would go with you."

"Oh, I don't want to go to Sunday school! I've never been there. I wouldn't know how to act," growled Stephen.

An expression of pain crossed Mrs. Tucker's face. She remembered the train experience and she again realized that she had failed her children in not giving them Christian training. Had she been a faithful mother, Stephen would never have spoken as he just did. But Mrs. Tucker's attention was distracted abruptly. Susan, who had been skipping along after the collie, suddenly tripped and fell flat on her face.

Dr. Tucker ran to pick her up from the leaves and brambles.

"Hurt?" he asked, setting her on her feet.

"No — but I'm scratched and dirty," complained Susan, brushing off her dress and rubbing her elbows with her handkerchief.

"Perhaps we had better walk more to the center of this clearing," suggested Mrs. Tucker. "Come over and walk with me, Susan."

Susan started to take a step toward her mother, but suddenly fell again.

"Susan," asked her mother anxiously, "what is wrong with you? Can't you stand up?"

"Something is tangled in my feet. It keeps tripping me," said Susan, as Stephen helped her to her feet.

Dr. Tucker pushed the leaves and underbrush aside with his foot. Caught on Susan's shoe was a stout cord.

"This is what it was," explained Dr. Tucker, holding up the cord. The string seemed to run back under the leaves, and Dr. Tucker pulled it.

"Wonder what it is?" Stephen kicked the leaves aside to follow the cord. "Looks as if it was buried with that collie's bone."

By this time, all the Tuckers were very much interested. They crowded around the cleared place where the collie had been digging. Stephen kept kicking the soft dirt with his foot. Dr. Tucker picked up a stick and began to poke in the hole.

"You pull, Stephen, while I loosen the earth," he instructed.

Stephen pulled, backing up as the cord lengthened.

"Look at this!" exclaimed Dr. Tucker, grabbing hold of a piece of white material and lifting it free from the dirt. "With all the talk in the papers lately, I would be tempted to say that we've found a parachute. But of course, that couldn't be."

Stephen and Dr. Tucker continued to draw the white material out of the deepening hole. The more

cloth that came free and unfolded before them the
more serious their faces became.

"Dad, I think it really is a parachute!" whistled
Stephen.

"Doesn't seem to be any doubt about it now," said
his father gravely. "This is something that the FBI
ought to know about. Looks as though we've stumbled on something mighty important."

"What will we do?" asked Mrs. Tucker, with concern, looking around her. "Do you suppose the person who hid it is still in the park?"

"No, I think it has been buried here for some time.
Maybe a month, I don't know. It is pretty well soaked
with moisture from the rain we've had," Dr. Tucker
said, shaking the loose dirt from the folds of the parachute.

"Imagine Japs dropping down right here in the park
— in parachutes," gasped Susan.

"Not Japs — Susan — Germans," Stephen corrected
her patiently.

"Germans are just as bad," Susan answered. "Maybe
worse."

"I think I'd better cut back home and telephone the
authorities about this. Stephen, you cover this thing
up with leaves and brush. The three of you had better
sit on that log over there and keep your eyes and ears
open. Don't tell anybody about this. If anybody
comes along and asks questions, tell him you're waiting for me. Keep up a conversation but don't mention this. It's serious business."

And Dr. Tucker hurried off through the trees.
They could hear him crashing down the hillside they
had just climbed a few moments before.

"What will we talk about?" asked Stephen, when he

had hidden the parachute under the leaves and covered it up so that the earth showed no evidence of having been disturbed.

"Let's see," said his mother, thinking a moment. "I'm afraid my mind is blank. I can't think of anything but what is over there under the leaves. I keep wondering where the person is who came down out of the air in it."

"Dad said not to talk about that," Stephen reminded her. "But it's all I can think of, too."

"I can think of something else," volunteered Susan.

"Good," said Stephen, "start in, quick."

"Miss Able read me from the Bible the other night the most interesting story I've ever heard. It was all about how God made the world, and the sea, and the moon, and the stars, and the sun, and trees and everything," began Susan. And so for the next half hour Susan told them all she could remember of what she had read of the Bible story of creation.

At first Stephen hardly listened, but as she went on he became more interested. Mrs. Tucker was interested from the very start.

"Never heard about it," said Stephen shortly.

"But it's true," declared Susan. "It is all in God's Book."

"Yes, I believe it is true," Mrs. Tucker agreed. "I heard that story when I was a little girl, younger than you, Susan."

"Why didn't you ever tell us, then?" asked Susan, wonderingly.

"I've not thought of it for a long time," her mother answered.

"I don't think I'll ever stop thinking about it," said Susan. "Why, God must be the most marvelous Person in the world — I guess I should say in heaven since that's where He lives, Miss Able says."

"That's right Susan, never stop remembering it. I can't tell you how sorry I'm becoming that I ever forgot it," her mother said seriously.

"I hear somebody coming," whispered Stephen, standing up.

"It must be Daddy," exclaimed Susan.

"It might not be, so we had better just sit still and wait," advised Stephen, seating himself.

After a few minutes, they could see Dr. Tucker coming through the trees accompanied by two men.

"Everything all right?" asked Dr. Tucker, when he came near enough to speak without raising his voice.

"Yes," answered Stephen. "No one came by."

"This is my wife, and my two children," explained Dr. Tucker. "These two men are from the FBI."

They all watched while Dr. Tucker showed the men the parachute and explained how they had stumbled upon it — rather how Susan had stumbled upon it — after the collie had dug around it for his bone. The men examined the parachute carefully, searched through the brush and the clearing. The Tuckers could hear them beating around in the bushes for some distance. And then they came back to the clearing where the Tuckers were waiting. One of them said:

"This is very important. Please don't tell anyone that you found this. We'll get some men over here and search every inch of these woods. There may be other clues as to where this person has gone. We will want your address, in case we want to get in touch with you later."

Dr. Tucker gave them their address, explaining it

was on the Broad Acres property, in back of the big house.

"Isn't that where the Misses Able live?" the younger of the two men asked.

"Why, yes," said Dr. Tucker. "Do you know the Misses Able?"

"Indeed, I do," the Federal agent responded cheerfully. "I bring them home from Sunday school and church in my car. Charming ladies, aren't they?"

Stephen looked with increased interest at the big, husky FBI agent, who represented a thrilling and exciting life to Stephen. What was it he had said about going to Sunday school?

"Do you go to Sunday school?" Stephen asked him impulsively.

The Federal agent laughed:

"I most certainly do. I've gone to Sunday school all my life. I never miss if I can help it."

All that evening until dark, the Tuckers could see figures moving in and out of the trees on the opposite hillside. They knew that there were government men going over the entire park, searching for clues which might help them apprehend the person who had come floating down out of the clouds in the parachute.

The next morning when Susan was ready to walk up to the Ables to go to Sunday school with them, Stephen said:

"I think I'll go with you. Do you 'spose there'd be room for me?"

14

LIGHT AND DARKNESS

Wasn't it exciting?" Susan settled herself comfortably in a wicker chair on the Ables' sun porch. "I was the one who found it. I mean, it got caught on my foot and made me fall. Did you ever see a *real* parachute — see it up close?"

Miss Able smiled and shook her head.

"No, I've only seen pictures of them. But my sisters, Miss Rebecca and Miss Rachel, have seen parachutes. They once visited a factory where they were being made."

"Wish I could see a factory like that sometime," said Susan with interest. "And when the FBI men came, there was one of them that said he knew you. His name was Frank Hardy."

"Yes, we know Frank Hardy very well," Miss Able acknowledged warmly. "He is a splendid young man and a real Christian. He goes to the same church we do."

"I guess I didn't see him there Sunday because he was hunting that man who came down in the parachute," suggested Susan. "Oh, I wanted to tell you all about it Sunday but we had to promise not to mention a word about it to anyone until the FBI said we could. I almost bursted."

Susan and Miss Able laughed together.

"Could we finish reading that story from the Bible this evening? Mother said I could stay until nine o'clock."

"I've kept all the crayons and pictures right here on the table, waiting for us." Miss Able drew her chair nearer. "Do you remember where we left off?"

"We stopped reading where it told about God making the sun and the moon and the stars. Aren't the stars — beautiful?" Susan remembered how wonderful they had seemed to her that night.

"The Psalmist tells us," Miss Able's face seemed to shine with an inner light as she spoke, "that the 'heavens declare the glory of God.' Every time we look up we are beholding some of God's glorious work."

"I think we begin at the place that said: 'And God said, Let the waters', don't we?" Susan asked after a pause.

"Yes, that's the verse. Would you like to read?"

Susan began to read, feeling almost as though this wonderful Book were partly hers:

"And God said, Let the waters bring forth abundantly the moving creature that hath life, and fowl that may fly above the earth in the open firmament of heaven. And God created great whales, and every living creature that moveth, which the waters brought forth abundantly, after their kind, and every winged fowl after his kind: and God saw that it was good. And God blessed them, saying, Be fruitful and multiply, and fill the waters in the seas, and let fowl multiply in the earth. And the evening and the morning were the fifth day."

"I believe we can use this last picture we drew," Miss Able said when Susan had finished reading. "What did God put into the world on the fifth day?"

Susan studied the verses carefully.

"He put the birds and creatures in the water."

"Yes, every winged fowl in the air and all kinds of fish in the seas," added Miss Able as she selected a colored pencil and began to sketch the outlines of several birds against the blue of the sky. "I'm not very good at drawing fish—but perhaps this one will look enough like a fish to give us the idea."

"But where are the animals?"

"We read about them in the next verse or two. Read on, Susan, and we'll add them to the picture also."

"And God said, Let the earth bring forth the living creature after his kind, cattle, and creeping thing, and beast of the earth after his kind: and it was so. And God made the beast of the earth after his kind, and cattle after their kind, and everything that creepeth upon the earth after his kind: and God saw that it was good."

"Those verses tell us of three general kinds of animals. What are they?" Miss Able wanted to know.

Susan wrinkled her eyebrows a moment and pondered over the verses.

"Well, it says cattle. That would be cows and sheep, I guess."

"Yes, cattle. What else?"

"Beasts."

"And one more."

"Creeping things," Susan continued. "What would they be?"

"Snakes, lizards, and that sort of animals. I'll just put in a sheep and a worm here. What other animal would you suggest, Susan?"

"A giraffe," Susan decided. "I'm very fond of giraffes."

"There!" Miss Able finished her drawing. "We have quite a full picture, haven't we?"

"God thought of everything, didn't He?" Susan marvelled.

"But there is still one thing missing from the picture."

"We could put more animals in," Susan thoughtfully suggested. "There aren't any monkeys in it."

"No, it's not an animal that's missing."

"Then I can't guess what it is," Susan's face looked blank.

Miss Able laughed.

"What do the next verses say?"

Susan read:

"And God said, Let us make man in our image, after our likeness: and let them have dominion over the fish of the sea, and over the fowl of the air, and over the cattle, and over all the earth, and over every creeping thing that creepeth upon the earth. So God created man in his own image, in the image of God created he him; male and female created he them."

"People!" Susan exclaimed.

Miss Able added two figures to the picture:

"Of course!" Miss Able agreed. "God made man and put him in charge of all the fish and birds and cattle and the whole earth. Man was the most important of all His creation. And you notice that God tells us that He made man 'in his own image.' There are some people who would want us to believe that man came from monkeys. But that isn't what God tells us."

"I read about that in a book one time. There were some awful looking pictures of hairy old men. It said that they were part like an ape and part like a man."

"I'm afraid they draw those pictures out of their imaginations. No one has ever actually seen one of those men. They find a few odd bones and then some scientist sits down and measures himself out a man."

"But," Susan insisted, "don't they know that God made man? Don't they have a Bible?"

"They know what the Bible says, but they will not believe it. They would rather make up their own stories to account for God's wonderful creation. When God made the first man and the first woman, He made them perfect human beings, strong and keen and handsome, I'm sure. Some other day soon we'll read all about Adam and Eve. We won't have time this evening. I'm afraid we'll have to hurry on if we are to get you home by nine o'clock. Let's read the rest of the verses telling about the sixth day."

Susan found the place and read:

"And God blessed them, and God said unto them, Be fruitful, and multiply, and replenish the earth, and subdue it: and have dominion over the fish of the sea, and over the fowl of the air, and over every living thing that moveth upon the earth. And God said, Behold, I have given you every herb bearing seed, which is upon the face of all the earth, and every tree, in which is the fruit of a tree yielding seed; to you it shall be for meat. And to every beast of the earth, and to every fowl of the air, and to every thing that creepeth upon the earth, wherein there is life, I have given every green herb for meat: and it was so. And God saw every thing that he had made, and, behold, it was very good. And the evening and the morning were the sixth day."

There were a number of difficult words in this passage, and Miss Able had to help.

"What does God say that man and all the animals are to eat for food?" she asked Susan.

After a moment, Susan answered:

"The fruit of trees and green herbs. Did they eat animals too, the way we do? Didn't they have any meat or chicken?"

"No, the first people on the earth were vegetarians. It was only many years later that they began to eat the flesh of animals."

"Were Adam and Eve the only people on the earth?"

"That's right. They are the parents of all of us," Miss Able assured her.

"Then we are all related, aren't we?" Susan seemed very pleased at the thought.

"Yes, we all belong to Adam's family. And just as Adam turned away from God's love and His law, all of Adam's children after him have followed in his steps. You know, Susan, God sees two families when He looks down upon us from heaven."

"Who are they?"

"Adam's family—the human family. And God's own family."

"Who belongs to God's family?"

"Everyone who opens his heart's door to God's Son, the Lord Jesus Christ, and receives Him into his heart and life to live, becomes a child of God. When God looks upon our hearts, He sees either Adam or Christ written there. Those who have Christ are called Christians."

"I never heard about this before," Susan said

thoughtfully. "Do you belong to God's family, Miss Able?"

"Yes, I do Susan. Not because I'm good or worthy of being His child. But because I have taken the Lord Jesus Christ to be my own personal Saviour. I'm trusting Him."

"That sailor we met on the train must belong to God's family, too," Susan thought out loud.

A clock chimed and Miss Able listened attentively until it finished:

"A quarter to nine," she announced. "We must hurry along if we are going to finish up tonight. There are only a few more verses."

Susan read:

"Thus the heavens and the earth were finished, and all the host of them. And on the seventh day God ended his work which he had made; and he rested on the seventh day from all his work which he had made. And God blessed the seventh day, and sanctified it: because that in it he had rested from all his work which God created and made."

"And so God finished His work," Miss Able concluded. "And He says that it was all perfect. There was no evil or sin or fear, sickness or sorrow or death in it."

Susan sat in quiet thought for a moment, and then asked:

"May I have those pictures to take home?"

"Indeed, you may, Susan. And I'll walk along home with you. It's rather a dark night."

Just as they were halfway down the sloping path, the lights at Haven House began to flicker and then suddenly went out.

"All the lights are out!" exclaimed Susan excitedly.

"Something must be wrong with the fuse box," Miss Able quickened her pace. "Let's hurry along and see if we can help."

Susan burst in the front door, calling:

"Mother! Daddy! What happened to the lights?"

"They just went out," Stephen informed her from the back of the house.

"It's all right, Susan. Just a fuse blown. If I can find my flashlight, I'll have it fixed in a second," Dr. Tucker was groping around in the dining room.

"But, John," Mrs. Tucker reminded him. "The flashlight won't work. You remember you promised to buy some new batteries last week."

"May I help you?" Miss Able offered from the front door.

"Oh, good evening, Miss Able," Mrs. Tucker greeted cordially. "I didn't know you were there. I'm sure we'll have the lights working in a minute. Do come in. I think we can find chairs in the dark. Watch the floor lamp here. I really ought to move it—it's too near the door for safety at times like these."

Dr. Tucker's voice spoke from the living room door: "Every single fuse blown!"

"What could have caused it?" asked Mrs. Tucker. "We weren't using any electrical equipment like the sweeper or washing machine. I can't understand it."

"Nor can I," Dr. Tucker responded. "It can't be the electricity generally for your lights are all on, Miss Able. And I can see other lights through the trees."

"Can't you fix it, Daddy?"

"That's part of the trouble. We have only one extra fuse."

"I'm sure we have some," Miss Able offered. "If

Stephen would run up to the house for them. Walter
undoubtedly could find several."

While they were waiting for Stephen to return
with the new fuses, Dr. Tucker remarked:

"There must be something wrong with our electric
system here. The bills have been entirely too large
for the amount we use. I'll have to have a serviceman
come out and go over the whole wiring arrangement
of the house."

Walter, the Able gardner and man-of-all-work, came
back with Stephen to see if he could be of any assist-
ance. In a few minutes, the new fuses installed, the
lights were on again. Dr. Tucker and Walter spent
some little time examining the fuse box and other
connections, but could not discover what it was that
had suddenly plunged the whole house into a forced
blackout.

"Well, I'll have a repairman come out tomorrow
morning," Dr. Tucker concluded as Miss Able and
Walter were leaving. "There's something wrong
somewhere."

And he was right!

15

THE THIRD WARNING

AFTER a day's shopping, Mrs. Tucker, the children, and Maggie had met Dr. Tucker at the office and all drove home together in the family car. The back seat was filled with Susan and bundles and Maggie. What a relief to get out of the hot town and into the cool park!

While Dr. Tucker parked the car in back of the house, Susan, Stephen, Maggie, and Mrs. Tucker loaded their arms with the packages they had spent the day purchasing. Mrs. Tucker, with one free hand, was jabbing at the keyhole and when the door swung open, they all trooped in, glad to be home once more. Dr. Tucker came in last with the remaining packages.

"Somebody dropped a piece of paper," he announced, balancing his bundles and stooping to pick up a sheet of paper from the floor.

"Put it on the table, please," called back Mrs. Tucker. "Must be the store list."

As Dr. Tucker threw the paper on the table, something about it made him pause. He put down his packages, and opened the folded paper. What he read made his jaw square and his eyes narrow. Mrs. Tucker came to the door:

"Is that the slip of paper? What is it John? Why so serious?"

"Because," said Dr. Tucker firmly, "if this is a joke, I don't think it is very funny."

"What?"

"This note. Read it." He handed over the paper.

Susan and Stephen came in while Mrs. Tucker was reading the paper.

"Something going on?" asked Stephen, throwing himself into a chair.

"John, what does all this mean?" asked Mrs. Tucker, looking startled.

"What, Mother? What's wrong?" asked Susan, alarmed.

"We seem to have another note," explained Dr. Tucker, "from somebody who is afraid to sign his name."

"What does it say?" Stephen sat up, all alert.

Dr. Tucker read:

"WE TRIED TO WARN YOU. DON'T BE FOOLS AND IGNORE THIS LAST WARNING. GET OUT OF THAT STABLE AND GET OUT OF WASH-INGTON. UNLESS YOU DO NOT VALUE YOUR LIVES."

"John," said Mrs. Tucker, sitting down weakly and looking a little pale. "I don't think that this is a joke. I think that the writer of that note is in earnest."

"I'm afraid you're right. We thought the telephone call was a college prank. I laughed at the note in my laundry box. But I'm beginning to wonder whether a practical joker would be so persistent, and so — threatening."

"What should we do?" asked Stephen, ready for action.

"Couldn't we call the police?" suggested Susan, a little frightened.

"'Scuse me, Miz Tucker, but didn't you say we wuz to have that chicken for supper tonight?" Maggie asked from the door, her hands wrapped in the folds of her white apron.

"Yes, I did, Maggie, I thought there would be plenty for tonight. Don't you think there's enough?"

"No, ma'am."

"Are you sure, Maggie? We talked about it this morning. There seemed to be plenty then."

"Yes, ma'am but dis morning there was *some*. To-night dey's nothin' but bones."

Mrs. Tucker looked at Stephen. But Stephen protested earnestly:

"I didn't Mother. I wasn't even in the kitchen today."

"Susan?"

"No, I didn't eat it."

"John?"

"If it was there this morning, how could I eat it? I've been at the office all day."

"I'll come out and see, Maggie." Mrs. Tucker followed Maggie out to the kitchen. In a few moments, Mrs. Tucker's voice was heard calling:

"John!"

"Yes." Dr. Tucker was already on his way to the kitchen. "Coming!"

The children followed close at his heels.

"John, it looks as if someone has been helping himself to our icebox. Not only the chicken is gone, but also that half of meringue pie is missing."

"Humm-m," said Dr. Tucker, trying not to alarm the family. "Wish I had thought of it first. Had my mouth all set for it."

"Do you suppose it could have been those tramps?" Mrs. Tucker looked a little nervous.

"Maybe you left the back door unlocked, Maggie,"

suggested Stephen, bending over to look at the ice box.

"No, it was locked," Mrs. Tucker assured him. "I tried it just before we left. Besides it's still locked."

"That's right," Stephen was examining the door.

"Whoever ate the chicken had dirty hands, that's certain," said Dr. Tucker pointing to a greasy smear on the white icebox.

"A fingerprint!" shouted Stephen.

"More of a hand smudge, I'd say," replied Dr. Tucker, as he kneeled on the floor to get a better view.

Mrs. Tucker put her hands to her head and shut her eyes.

"Tramps! White handkerchiefs. Parachutes! Lights out! Now chicken and pie stolen, mysterious notes— if one more thing happens I shall — I shall — faint!" she declared desperately.

Just then a loud thump was heard upstairs.

And Mrs. Tucker fainted.

For a moment, no one knew what to do. Dr. Tucker looked at Mrs. Tucker crumpled in Maggie's arms and then at the ceiling. Maggie cried:

"You all go upstairs. I'll take care of Miz Tucker."

Dr. Tucker and Stephen both ran for the stairs.

"Be careful now, Stephen, you stay behind me," Dr. Tucker warned.

Upstairs they searched every room and clothes press but found no one. The only thing out of the ordinary was in Dr. and Mrs. Tucker's bedroom where they found a chair upset in the middle of the floor.

"I don't understand what could have caused that noise," Dr. Tucker stood puzzled in the middle of the room.

"Must have been this chair," Stephen said, setting it up.

"Chairs don't overturn without help," persisted Dr. Tucker.

"Well," Stephen suggested, "it might have been sort of half falling over all day and then suddenly fell clear over."

"Might have," said Dr. Tucker doubtfully.

"Just has to be," insisted Stephen. "You don't believe in ghosts, do you?"

"No," laughed Dr. Tucker. "I suppose it must have fallen over of its own accord. Though I still say it's strange."

Downstairs, Maggie and Susan had gotten Mrs. Tucker into the living room and on the couch. She was feeling better by the time Dr. Tucker and Stephen returned, and was a bit ashamed when they explained it was only a chair that had fallen over.

"But I do think I ought to report this note to the police," said Dr. Tucker. "It may not mean anything. But, if I turn it over to the police, they can worry about it instead of us."

And so the next morning, Dr. Tucker stopped by the police station and had a talk with the officer in charge. He told him about the telephone call before they left College Hill, the note in the laundry box, and this last note which they had found under their front door.

"I don't like to seem foolish reporting this," explained Dr. Tucker apologetically, "but it is making my wife nervous, and after all, there just might be something in back of it."

"Entirely right," the officer assured him. "We'll look into it. Let us know if anything else should happen."

"Oh, yes," Dr. Tucker remembered as he was leaving the station. "At the same time we found the note, we also discovered that someone had been enjoying our icebox. They left a greasy smear on the outside of it."

"I'll send someone out to look at it," said the policeman, making a note. "That might be a clue."

"I only hope that Maggie hasn't washed it off. I'd better telephone right away, and ask them to preserve it," said Dr. Tucker.

But before he reached Mrs. Tucker by telephone, Maggie had cleaned off the smear. Indeed, she had thoroughly scrubbed and disinfected the whole icebox, and was in the process of washing down the walls.

"Don't know what kind of germs that thief brought in," she was grumbling under her breath.

"I'm afraid," smiled Dr. Tucker, to the police officer, "that we are not up on the ways of crime in our house. We shall certainly try to do better next time we have a clue."

16

THE MAN IN THE TREE

STEPHEN had spent the afternoon in the Smithsonian Institute and was hiking home. To save time, for he knew dinner would be waiting, he took a short cut through the park. At the top of a hill, from which he could see the chimney of Haven House, he stopped a moment to slip on his coat. There was no path and he would need both arms to balance himself as he scrambled down the steep bank. Just as he was ready to plunge, his eye caught sight of something in a tree just below. His heart turned over. There was a man perched in the top of the tree, halfway down the hill. His back was to Stephen. He was waving a large white handkerchief in slow and regular movements.

Stephen crouched behind some bushes and watched the strange man. It looked as though he was signalling. Perhaps he was a surveyor, thought Stephen, suddenly feeling silly hiding behind the bushes. He was probably a government surveyor giving directions to other surveyors. Finding that parachute the other day made everything look mysterious. Stephen was getting ready to stand up and plunge down the hill toward home. He had decided to pretend that he had not seen the man in the tree. At that moment the man turned and cast a hasty glance around him.

Suddenly Stephen felt cold all over. His heart pounded. He knew the man. It was the same man who had fallen against him in the train, who had mumbled something in German. What was he doing? Stephen thought of the parachute again. Maybe this man had something to do with the parachute. Maybe he was signalling to the man who had come down in the parachute. Stephen kept his eyes fastened on him. Methodically the man continued to wave the white cloth. Then he stuffed the cloth in his pocket and raised field glasses to his eyes. Stephen suddenly wished he had learned signalling. He was sorry he had not joined the Scouts. He began to realize how many things there were to know in the world and how few he knew. One thought after another flashed through his mind.

The man in the tree cast another furtive glance around him, and then agilely slid down the tree. On the ground, he paused long enough to brush off his clothes with the large white handkerchief and rub the black from the tree off his hands. Then he turned and walked quickly to the right. It was just beginning to get dark. Stephen watched the man hurry away. What should he do? Stephen felt that somehow this man was mixed up in all the queer things that had happened lately. This was the first person that had been seen. If he got away now they might never see him again. The parachute man might escape. Stephen decided to follow him. The path at the foot of the hill, along which the mysterious stranger was walking, circled the hill and led on to the road. Stephen began to walk quickly and as quietly as he could along the ridge above the path in the same direction as the stranger.

In a few minutes he caught sight of the man again. His heart beating double time, Stephen followed along behind as closely as he dared. The lower path soon joined the highway and the man turned on to it, walking briskly. Stephen continued to follow the stranger from the top of the ridge. If the man should suddenly dart off the road, he would certainly lose sight of him. He wondered how he would ever get down to the road without being heard. The twigs on the ground would surely snap and call the stranger's attention to him.

Just then two big buses turned the curve of the road and came "snorting" by. They were filled with young people, who were hanging out of the windows, laughing and singing. Surely the noise of the motors and the voices would drown out the sound of Stephen's crashing down the hillside. As he plunged down the embankment, some of the girls in the bus saw him and waved and shouted.

"Girls are such dumbbells," Stephen growled through his teeth, dodging bushes and branches which stung his face and tore at his clothes.

However, the hurrying figure of the stranger did not turn around. He did not even stop to let the buses go by, but merely stepped off the side of the road. After they had passed, he stepped back on to the road and continued to walk rapidly down the road, with Stephen following.

Stephen had read in books about people following others. He had often tried to imagine what it would be like. And here he was, following someone who might be a dangerous spy. Stephen was scared. His back felt creepy, but he kept right on. He was glad he had worn tennis shoes for they made practically no noise. The man apparently was headed out of the Park. Stephen knew that this road led into a main thoroughfare which ran through the park, near one of the entrances to the Zoo. At the corner of the road and the cross street, there was an old deserted mill named Flint Mill. It had been there when the city of Washington was not much more than mud roads and a few houses.

As the stranger approached the crossroads, he stopped. Traffic was coming from both directions, but none was turning into the park. The man waited until the lights from the passing automobiles had sped by. For a moment, after the glare of the bright lights, Stephen could not see the stranger. Where had he disappeared? Stephen hurried forward. As he came up to the Mill, Stephen heard a noise like knocking on hollow wood; then a creak and — silence!

"He's gone into the Mill," Stephen said to himself, creeping near to the side of the building.

Pressing his ear to the door, he heard noises inside. If only he could hear what they were saying! If only he could get inside without being seen! Stephen forgot his fear in the excitement of the moment. He edged slowly around the Mill but found no other opening. The few windows were nailed shut. The Mill had not been used for years.

As he tiptoed back toward the front door again, he heard it open. Stephen flattened himself against the side of the Mill scarcely daring to breathe. He heard the patter of soft footsteps. It sounded like two people.

"Well, we've got to get that stuff out of there, that's all there is to it," said a voice in an undertone. "And we've got to get it out right away. Ernest is there now, getting it ready."

"Try my suggestion first. If that doesn't work— well, we'll have to use yours. Though it's dangerous," another voice replied in the same guarded tones.

"This thing has been delayed weeks now. The

Chief won't listen to any more excuses. Well, let me know."

And the two figures hurried down the road together and crossed over to a picnic parking ground. In a few seconds, Stephen could see the dark shapes of two cars slip silently on to the road. They turned in opposite directions and disappeared in the night. Stephen's heart was beating wildly. When the sound of their motors had died away, he slipped out of the shadows of the Mill and began to run for home.

17

THE INVITATION

STEPHEN, we were so worried. Why, you're out of breath. You've been running!" said Mrs. Tucker when Stephen burst into the house.

"And your dinner's cold," chimed in Susan.

"Ran all the way home," he gasped, throwing himself on the couch. "Where's Dad?"

"Here I am," said Dr. Tucker, coming in. "What's up? Just beginning to wonder where you were."

Still breathing heavily, Stephen began to tell about the man in the tree with the field glasses and the white cloth; and how he followed him down the road; about the second man in the Mill; and what he had heard them say and how they had slipped silently away into the night.

"Stephen, what if they had caught you!" exclaimed Mrs. Tucker in a frightened tone. "You don't know what they would have done to you."

"But they didn't catch me," Stephen grinned. "And now we know that fellow we saw in the train is mixed up in this business some way."

"I think there is more in back of this than we suspect," said Dr. Tucker thoughtfully. "We seem to have stumbled into something. It's beginning to look like a hornet's nest."

"I think you ought to call Frank Hardy at once and tell him," insisted Mrs. Tucker.

"I'll go by his office in the morning," Dr. Tucker

assured here. "There's no use bothering him tonight. There's nothing he can do now. The men have gone, and undoubtedly will not be back this way any more tonight."

That night Stephen dreamed that he was chasing a German spy up and down the park hills. Each time he was about to grab the spy, Susan caught hold of his coat and slowed him down.

The next morning at breakfast Stephen viewed Susan with disgust as he remembered the dream which had seemed so real he felt that it had been Susan's fault the spy had escaped.

Maggie brought in the morning mail to the breakfast table. Among other letters, there was an invitation from Mrs. Madison asking Mrs. Tucker, Susan and Stephen to come to lunch that very day.

"How nice of Mrs. Madison," Mrs. Tucker exclaimed. "We really should invite *her* — but it's just like her to ask us first. Would you like to go, children?"

"Oh, yes," Susan beamed.

"I could finish looking at those confederate war books," Stephen remarked practically.

With eyebrows screwed at angles, Dr. Tucker looked at Stephen.

"Remember your manners, Stephen."

Since it was Maggie's day off, they decided to drive Dr. Tucker to the office early, spend the morning at the Art Gallery and be at Mrs. Madison's about twelve-thirty o'clock in good time for lunch. They had to be back home before three o'clock, since the butcher was delivering some meat, and it must not be left out in the hot sun. They would not be able to wait for Dr. Tucker that evening.

Mrs. Tucker left her husband at the Department of Justice, where he was to see Mr. Hardy. The car parked in a lot, Mrs. Tucker and the children spent the morning enjoying the sights at the new Art Gallery. They were so interested that time passed more quickly than they realized.

"Oh, we'll have to hurry along if we are not going to be late for lunch!" Mrs. Tucker looked at her watch. "We'll come back another time to see the other pictures."

But when they presented themselves at the door of Mrs. Madison's house, they had to ring the bell a half dozen times before they got any response. The front door, usually open, was closed and the screen door was fastened.

"Mrs. Madison *must* be at home. I hardly think my watch is more than ten minutes fast, at the most." Mrs. Tucker put her wrist watch to her ear to make sure it was going.

"Here comes somebody. I can hear footsteps," said Susan, cocking her head to one side.

They could hear someone unlocking the door. And then it was opened a few inches. Through the crack they could see the brown face of Mrs. Madison's maid, her jaw swathed in a bulky bandage.

"Yas'm?" she said, with her eyes half shut and her face twisted.

"Are you sick, Beulah?" asked Mrs. Tucker kindly.

"Yas'm." Beulah answered, still not opening the door more than a few inches.

"Is Mrs. Madison at home? I believe she is expecting us?"

"No'm. Not till Tuesday."

"That's strange," said Mrs. Tucker, wonderingly.

"Yas'm. 'Tis strange," agreed Beulah, absently closing the door a fraction of an inch.

"Well, please tell Mrs. Madison that Mrs. Tucker called. I'll get in touch with her later. I hope you'll feel better, Beulah."

"Yas'm, thank you ma'am. Same to you."

"Maybe she said *next* Wednesday," suggested Stephen, as they got into the car.

"I'm certain she said today. The invitation definitely said she hoped that its lateness wouldn't mean that we would be unable to come. Stephen and Susan," said Mrs. Tucker with firmness, "I don't like this."

"Maybe Mrs. Madison didn't send the invitation at all," suggested Stephen recalling the recent strange events.

"I'm sure she didn't," Mrs. Tucker replied.

"Then who did?" asked Stephen.

"Or why did they?" added Mrs. Tucker.

"It was mean," said Susan.

"What will we do now," asked Stephen. "Go back to the Art Gallery?"

"No," said Mrs. Tucker, "I think we had better go home."

And so they turned the car toward Haven House. They rode in silence until, just after they entered the park, the front wheel began to wobble in a peculiar manner. Mrs. Tucker slowed the car.

"Something's wrong with the car," said Mrs. Tucker. "I wonder if it could be a flat tire."

She drove the car to the side of the road and Stephen got out to look.

"It's flat on the bottom, all right," he called back to his mother. "Guess we'll have to change it."

"Oh, dear," cried Mrs. Tucker. "I just knew something like this would happen! Your father took the spare out of the car last night. He didn't put it back!"

"Where is it? In back of the house?" asked Stephen.

"Yes," answered his mother. "We do seem to be having our troubles today, don't we?"

"I can run home and get it," said Stephen, taking off his coat. "You wait here. It won't take me long."

And off he ran.

18

TRAPPED!

STEPHEN approached Haven House from the back, running at a dog's trot. Just as he was bounding across the last few yards to the rear of the house, where he could see the tire leaning against the wall, he was amazed to see a man come from the direction of the front door and hurry off toward the wooded section nearest to the house. The man was carrying a heavy box. Who was the man? It didn't look like the butcher. Besides the butcher would probably park his car in the driveway. The man was going in the wrong direction. He was headed into the woods. Stephen stepped quickly around the corner of the house, where he could watch the man who was disappearing from sight among the trees. Stephen heard the front screen door bang. Another man, also carrying a heavy box, followed the first into the woods.

Stephen started. The second man was — yes — was the man of the train and the tree and the mill! What were they doing in Haven House? What was in those boxes? Maybe they were stealing books or silverware. Stephen waited until the second man was lost from sight among the trees. Avoiding the path and running as quietly as he could, Stephen hurried after the two men. In a few minutes, just ahead, on the bridle path, Stephen saw the two men and a car. One was putting a box into the trunk compartment. The other had rested his on the fender. Their backs were to

Stephen. Suddenly a twig snapped under Stephen's feet. One of the men jumped, almost upsetting the box he was balancing.

"What was that?" his voice was hoarse.

"Don't be so nervous," the other man answered. "Probably a squirrel. You know these woods are full of them."

After putting both boxes in the car, the men turned back toward Haven House. Stephen, crouched behind a tree, waited until they could no longer be seen and then crept cautiously toward the car and peered into it. In the back seat he could see some kind of a radio and three or four boxes. One box was marked "Explosives." The radio didn't belong to the Tuckers, nor had Stephen ever seen the boxes before. Apparently they were not stealing the Tuckers' possessions. But from where were they getting these things? They were bringing the boxes out of Haven House.

The men would be back in a few minutes. Perhaps this would be their last trip. How could Stephen stop them? They mustn't get away. Stephen wished he had his air rifle. If he could only get word to his father and to Frank Hardy. What should he do?

Perhaps he could fix the car so that it wouldn't go. Then they would be stuck there. Stephen, casting a glance behind, raised the hood of the car. The motor looked so complicated! He would have to break something that they couldn't fix. But Stephen didn't know what that would be. Impulsively he reached in and grabbed several wires and pulled. At first they held. Suddenly they broke loose and Stephen almost fell over backwards. He jammed them into his pocket. Was that enough? Maybe the car could go without the wires.

"If they don't catch me and skin me alive," Stephen murmured to himself, "I'm going to learn all about cars, beginning tomorrow."

The men must be due back any moment. He could not risk waiting another second. Quickly he closed the hood of the engine and darted back among the trees. Skirting from the path he ran as lightly as he could toward the house. Some yards to his left he heard footsteps pounding along the path. And then a few minutes later, a second pair of footsteps.

Once out of the woods, Stephen raced for the house. Inside a hasty glance around the first floor showed nothing disturbed. He ran to the telephone to call his father, but he could not get the usual buzzing dial tone. Something was wrong with the telephone.

Stephen ran up the stairs two at a time, to the second floor. The first thing Stephen saw as he reached the upper hall was a chair standing in the center of Dr. and Mrs. Tucker's room. Inside the door, Stephen stopped in his tracks. His mouth fell open. His jaw sagged in amazement.

There hanging from an opening in the ceiling was a rope ladder! The men were carrying the boxes down from the space between the roof and the ceiling! Stephen had never known there was an opening to the loft for it had been neatly concealed in the oak panels of the ceiling. As he gazed at the gaping hole, he suddenly realized that they must be planning to return or they wouldn't have left the trapdoor open.

But what was up there? Did he dare look? Hesitating for a moment, he rashly grabbed the end of the rope ladder and pulled himself up until his head was inside the opening. At first he could not see anything in the pitch darkness. And then his eyes began to make out piles of boxes like the ones already in the car outside. And guns! Even one that was mounted and looked like a machine gun. There were blankets, a stove, and dozens of other things at which he did not take the time more than to glance.

"Saboteurs!" Stephen exclaimed aloud. "This must be where that parachute fellow was hiding. Right in our house!"

He felt cold all over, and a little sick. Quickly he dropped down the ladder. They would be coming back any minute. Somehow he must keep them here until he could get word to the police. How could he do it? They would not be afraid of him. They could get rid of him easily. Stephen remembered the stormy night he had been thrown down the stairs. If only the family were home. If only his father were here. The two of them might be able to trap the intruders while Mother and Susan ran for help. But the family wasn't home. Mother and Susan were sitting up the road peacefully waiting for him, little dreaming how desperately he needed their help. He thought of the big house. Maybe he could run up there and telephone for help. But what if they left before he got back; or if they saw him through the little round opening in the side of the loft that faced the big house (it had always reminded Stephen of a port hole on a ship), they might shoot him.

But they were coming back now. He could see them, half running, hurrying down the path from the woods.

Stephen dived for the stairs, and slid down the bannister. As he flung himself behind the divan in the living room, the first man ran into the hallway. Stephen could feel the walls tremble as they stamped upstairs. He could hear them grunt as they pulled themselves up through the hole in the rafters. He heard the chair scrape and fall over. He remembered the evening they all had heard the same sound and his mother had fainted. If they had known then that German spies were in the house!

But he must keep them here. How? If only the family would come home. If only his mother and sister would get tired waiting and come along to see what was keeping him. If only the Misses Able would come to call. Or Maggie come back. Or anybody, even the butcher boy. And then Stephen remembered something. If the men in the loft *thought* the entire Tucker family was at home, it would be just as though they were. They wouldn't dare to come down then!

Squirming out from in back of the couch, Stephen ran over to the phonograph. Where were the recordings they had made of the entire family last Christmas at College Hill? If he played them on the phonograph as loudly as he could, perhaps the men upstairs would think the family *had* returned. Stephen piled on three records and set the automatic change. He turned it on and then quietly slipped out the front door. Feeling a bit weak in the knees as the record began to play, Stephen thumped in and out of the house, fervently hoping it sounded like several people. He talked to himself, and laughed heartily, as naturally as possible and at the top of his voice, and he tried to enter into the conversation on the records.

"I hope they can hear up there," he muttered.

In and out of the living room, from the hall, to the kitchen he pranced. He kept calling things to Susan, asking his father questions, pretending to answer his mother. The records played on merrily. There was laughing and talking and joking. His father was singing a funny song. They all clapped.

While the phonograph records whirled on, Stephen again went to the telephone and jiggled the receiver up and down. There was still no response. The line was dead. Back he went to his tramping over the floor. He wondered how long he could keep this up. Suddenly he remembered the machine gun and wondered if the men might not decide to shoot their way out. Shaking with a chill, back and forth through the rooms he marched, clattering dishes, running water in the kitchen sink, even getting out his cornet and tooting a bit on that.

Wouldn't anyone ever come home? His mother was always worrying about him when nothing was wrong. Now that something was wrong and he needed somebody to worry, no one seemed to care at all. Oh, if somebody would only come! He kept going to the front door to look out.

Suddenly his heart began to sing. There was his father hurrying down the path.

"Father!" Stephen shouted above the noise of the phonograph.

For a moment he was frozen with fear. His heart almost stopped beating. What if the men upstairs began to shoot at his father from the porthole? But then he remembered that the house was supposed to be full of people. If they had been going to shoot, they surely would have done it fifteen or twenty minutes ago — or was it two hours? Stephen couldn't remember. It seemed like years since he had turned on the phonograph and started stamping up and down through the house. And now his father was coming.

Stephen ran to the door to meet him. With his finger to his lips, he pointed upstairs. His father nodded and stepped into the house.

"Thank God, you are alive and safe," he gripped Stephen by the shoulders. "Maggie phoned me."

"They're upstairs," Stephen whispered, though the babble of voices on the phonograph records would have drowned out even an ordinary tone. "I played the records so they would think the whole family was home."

"We've got to get out of here," Dr. Tucker pulled Stephen by the arm. "Turn off that phonograph and come on."

"But what about them? They'll get away," urged Stephen.

"That's just what we want," Dr. Tucker urged. "Hurry. There's no time to lose."

Dr. Tucker turned off the phonograph, and then said in a loud voice:

"If we don't hurry, we'll be late. Come along everybody."

And then, beckoning Stephen to do the same, Dr. Tucker tramped out of the house with much noise, quietly hurried back in, and stamped out again. Outside the second time, he half dragged Stephen to the rear of the house, the side farthest from the porthole. Once away from the house, Dr. Tucker and Stephen started to run. Bewildered, a hundred questions running through his mind, Stephen kept calling back to his father:

"But they'll get away!"

"Yes, yes!" said his father. "Hurry! Faster!"

19

SOLVED!

BUT the thing that I couldn't understand," said Stephen, "was that the more I told Dad that they would escape, the faster he insisted we run."

"But you understand now," answered Dr. Tucker, "that we felt they were desperate enough to take a chance at shooting their way out. No one was at home at the Ables. There were no other close neighbors. Folks who did hear the shooting probably would have thought it was the back firing of passing cars."

Mrs. Tucker, Susan, Frank Hardy, Dr. Tucker and Stephen were seated in the living room of Haven House (with Maggie hovering at the door) talking over the exciting events of the past few hours.

"Well, I must confess," said Mrs. Tucker, "it is all too much for me. I don't understand it. I hope one of you will explain. It's like a jig-saw puzzle with pieces missing."

"Perhaps we can supply those missing pieces for you," offered Frank Hardy, the young Government agent.

"I wish you would," smiled Mrs. Tucker.

"I'm sure we all would like to know the full story," added Dr. Tucker.

"Well," began Frank Hardy, "last year we started to trace down a gang of foreign agents who were causing all sorts of trouble and destruction to our wartime

program. They seemed to be so clever that it looked
as if we might never catch them. One of their favorite
and milder tricks was to send notes warning men and
women not to come to Washington to take war work.
Some of the people who got these threatening letters
were timid and did not come to Washington. Others
came and turned the notes over to us."

"Well, that explains the notes you got, John," said
Mrs. Tucker. "It wasn't a college prank after all."

"And the phone call," Stephen put in.

"We knew that they had headquarters in Washing here," continued Mr. Hardy. "And we knew
some of the less important members of the gang. But
we wanted the head man. We knew they had a high-
powered radio set; but we could not seem to discover
their hiding place."

"Now, I'm beginning to see why our electric lights
were blown out," commented Dr. Tucker. "Too much
load on the current."

Susan looked a little frightened: "To think that
all the time they were right here in this house! God
certainly took care of us, didn't He?"

"He did, indeed, Susan," agreed Mr. Hardy. "But
these men did not stay here all the time. They used
the loft to keep their supplies, to hide any members
of the gang who were suspected by the Government
until they could get them out of town, and also to be
a sort of receiving station for those that were dropped
from planes in parachutes. When you came out here
that night of the storm, you caught them just leaving.
You thought they were tramps, and they thought you
were tramps. However, when Mr. Bell and Dr.
Tucker came out and inspected the place, and then
the exterminators came out, they began to suspect

that the long-deserted stable was going to be put into use."

"If anybody was up in the loft while the exterminators were using that ghastly chemical," grinned Stephen, "I'm sure they got an awful headache."

Mrs. Tucker looked triumphantly at her husband.

"I never did believe that tramps carried clean, white handkerchiefs!"

"Well, we weren't far wrong on the rats, though. You could almost call spies — rats — human rats," returned Dr. Tucker.

"Of course," went on Mr. Hardy, "when Susan tripped over the parachute our attention was turned to the park more than ever. When the gang saw our men searching the park and with you folks living in the stable — I mean Haven House — they knew that they would have to move their things out right away before they would be discovered. It was getting to be a much too dangerous hiding place. Besides, they never could be sure of getting at them when they were needed. The only time members of the gang could get in or out of the loft was when you were away. Once or twice, apparently, when you came home unexpectedly, they were trapped. They seemed to keep a little food on hand, but I'm sure it was mighty uncomfortable and risky."

"I guess they thought that we might be scared out by that note they left under the door," suggested Stephen.

"That's what they hoped to do," agreed Mr. Hardy. "They were really desperate. They couldn't very well make use of their radio set when you were at home, and their chief was getting impatient. They either had to get rid of you or get their supplies out of the loft."

"That's what they were talking about that night at the Mill," Stephen sat forward in his chair.

"Yes, and your man in the tree had been signalling instructions to one of the gang who was trapped in the rafters," Mr. Hardy went on.

"And Mrs. Madison did *not* send us an invitation to lunch," exclaimed Mrs. Tucker.

"No," laughed Mr. Hardy. "That was another unsuccessful attempt to get you all out of the house. They knew that Dr. Tucker would be at the office, and somehow they knew that Wednesday was Maggie's day off. They thought that by sending you that invitation, they would have an opportunity to carry their supplies out of the house unhindered. Indeed, they hoped that you would never know about their ever having used the loft at all."

"But Mrs. Madison wasn't home. That didn't help them," Susan insisted.

"They didn't know that. There's always some slip that criminals do not count on. They thought that you would go to Mrs. Madison's around lunchtime, and Mrs. Madison would be forced to invite you to stay."

"How embarrassing," protested Mrs. Tucker.

"In any event, they hoped that you would be away long enough for them to get their supplies out of the house," Mr. Hardy paused for a moment.

"But," Mrs. Tucker smiled grimly, "they did not count on my being so provoked at the practical joke that I decided to come straight home."

"It was you, Susan," Stephen remembered suddenly, "who insisted that the German on the train wasn't a spy."

"Well, he might not have been," defended Susan.

"But he was," Stephen reminded her. "*I* was right."

"They had another problem they hadn't counted on," continued Mr. Hardy. "Maggie usually went off on her holiday about 10:30 o'clock. They had someone watching the house to give the "all clear" signal. When Maggie cut her finger and didn't have any bandage, she went up to the Ables to borrow some from Arbutus. When the watcher saw her leave Haven House, he quite naturally thought she had started on her holiday. That was about 11:00 o'clock. Had Maggie returned immediately upon getting the bandage, the watcher would have realized his mistake. But she stayed to talk with Arbutus until about 12:30 when she hurried back to Haven House here hoping to catch the grocer's truck in time to get a ride into town. Of course, by this time, the two men were in the house in the midst of transporting their stock of destructive supplies. Just as Maggie got to the back door of the house, she heard footsteps coming down from the second floor. As she got to the kitchen door, to her amazement she saw two strange men go out the front door carrying large boxes."

"Almos' fainted," Maggie murmured from the doorway, her eyes rolling.

"I wouldn't wonder," Mrs. Tucker agreed with her.

"Well, Maggie scampered out the back door and up to the Able house. She and Arbutus between them telephoned Dr. Tucker. We had already had a talk in the morning about the strange things that were happening around Haven House. We both felt that somehow all of these mysterious events were connected with the gang of saboteurs. So when Maggie telephoned Dr. Tucker, he immediately called me. In five minutes, I had picked up Dr. Tucker in a car

and we were on our way. There were twelve of us
in three cars."

"And found Susan and me along the road with a
very flat tire," put in Mrs. Tucker.

Dr. Tucker took up the story here:

"When I learned that Stephen had gone to the house
for the spare tire, I was afraid that he might have
been caught by these unscrupulous men. I believed
that if I went up to the house alone they would not be
too alarmed at seeing me, and if they had captured
Stephen they probably would put me in the same place
they had him."

"They might have shot you both," said Mrs. Tucker
with a shudder.

"Then, too," added Mr. Hardy, "we didn't want to
close in on them too soon. Maggie said she had seen
only two of them. We were hoping they might lead
us to their chief; he was the one we wanted. If we
had tried to shoot it out with them near the house,
Stephen might have gotten hurt. We felt sure they
had plenty of ammunition and probably could have
held out for a long time. Your house would have
been ruined, and we might have lost some of our men.
So we encircled the house, hiding in the woods, and
waited. When they thought that the house was again
empty they began to carry out the remaining things."

"But they couldn't have used their car," grinned
Stephen.

"Why not?" asked Susan.

"Because I pulled these out of the engine," Stephen
exhibited the wires which he had stuffed into his
pocket.

They all laughed.

"Stephen," Mr. Hardy congratulated him, "you'll make a good FBI agent."

"I'd certainly like to be one," Stephen answered earnestly.

"Well, get a good education, live a clean, honest life, and perhaps one day you can. And the best way I know to live the kind of life which has no question marks or dark spots on it is by becoming a Christian," Mr. Hardy advised. "And, of course, faithfully attending Sunday school and church."

"But how *did* you catch them?" Susan wanted to know.

"Just as we hoped. Evidently the chief had gotten word that the Government was closing in on them. A second car travelling at a breakneck speed swooped up the bridle path. There were three men in it. When they discovered that something was wrong with the loaded car, they decided to abandon it with all of the things in it. They were anxious only to save their own skins by this time. We were waiting for them down the road. They tried to shoot their way through, but we caught them all. One of the three men in the second car was the chief. So it was well that we waited," concluded Mr. Hardy. "I think that's about everything. And the Department of Justice is deeply grateful for the fine help and cooperation that you all gave to us."

"Just think," pouted Maggie, "dat tasty bit of meringue pie and all dat chicken eaten by a German spy! Glad I scoured dat kitchen good."

She bustled off to the kitchen, amid laughter, to make some ice tea and sandwiches.

"My, it's nice and peaceful around here?" sighed Susan.

20

SUSAN OPENS THE DOOR

THE next Sunday morning found Susan and Stephen and Mrs. Tucker in Sunday school. It was the first time in years that Mrs. Tucker had been inside of a church. She had gone this Sunday because she felt she needed to go. Stephen had gone because Mr. Hardy was going to be there. But Susan had gone because she liked it. As all the classes came together for the closing session, it was Frank Hardy, the assistant superintendent, who took charge.

"This morning," said Frank Hardy, looking very fresh in his white suit, "I want to tell you about four important things: a door, a knock, an ear, and a voice. I'm going to read you just one verse from the Word of God. It is found in Revelation 3:20:

"Behold, I stand at the door, and knock; if any man hear my voice, and open the door, I will come in to him, and will sup with him, and he with me.

"First, the door. This verse says, 'Behold, I stand at the door.' It is the Lord Jesus standing at the door. And the door is the door of our hearts. Each of us has a door with a latch on the inside. God wants us to open that door and let the Lord Jesus in. Satan wants us to keep it shut tight. This verse from God's Word tells us that 'Behold,' the Lord Jesus is standing at the door of our hearts this morning — right now, waiting to be let in. It is the same Lord Jesus who loves each one of us, who died to win us to God.

Just think of it: the very Son of God is standing outside of your heart — waiting, waiting.

"And then the verse says, 'and knock'. Not only is the Lord Jesus standing outside of the heart, waiting patiently, but He is knocking. He wants to come in. He longs to come in to live. How long shall we keep the Lord Jesus Christ waiting outside of our heart's door — knocking?

"This verse also tells us that if 'any man hear' his voice. Can you hear this morning? Do you have ears? Did you hear me read the verse from the Bible? Did you hear me when I read: 'Behold, I stand at the door, and knock; if any man hear my voice, and open the door, I will come in to him, and will sup with him, and he with me'? Do you hear?

"It is the voice of the Lord Jesus speaking. It is not my voice — I only read it to you. It is a message from the Lord Jesus Christ sent directly to you — to each one — to you and to me. His sweet voice is saying: 'Open the door of your heart and let me in this morning'. Do you hear Him call? The Lord Jesus loves you this morning. What do we do when someone who loves us knocks at our door and asks us to let him come in?"

It was Susan who answered, her eyes shining:

"We open the door and let him in!"

"Yes, Susan. We open the door and say: Come in! And so this morning, as the Lord Jesus is standing outside of the heart's door, knocking, waiting, calling to each one of us to open to Him, let us answer Him. Let us say 'Oh, Lord Jesus, I do open the door of my heart to you right now. Come into my heart, Lord Jesus, come in today.' Will you let Him in?"

And Susan did — at that very moment.